CW00400771

# THE HANGMAN'S
# DAUGHTER

ROSIE DARLING

# CHAPTER 1

*G*race Dillingham was huddled in the corner of her classroom, listening to the school master's footsteps echo between the desks.

*Click, click, click...*

The sound made her heartbeat race.

The schoolmaster was a tall, dark-haired bear of a man who had terrified Grace since her first day at Saint Mary's two years ago. He was perhaps the tallest man Grace had ever seen – taller even than her papa – and he seemed to wear the same long, black greatcoat whether the sun was blazing or the ground was white with snow. His voice was impossibly deep and rough, and Grace was sure she had never seen him smile.

The master's footsteps clicked past her and she felt the muscles in her shoulders tighten. She kept her eyes fixed on her slate, carefully copying out the sums on the blackboard at the front of the classroom. Although she did not dare to look at him, she could feel the master's eyes on her as she carefully formed the numbers. She felt her fingers tremble a little. Finally, the footsteps continued past her desk and Grace exhaled deeply in relief. She dared a glance to her left and noticed that the master had stopped beside the desk of her friend Phillip.

"What do you call this, Mr Butler?" the master boomed.

"My sums, sir." Phillip's voice was tiny. Grace felt a pang of sympathy. She knew how the schoolmaster scared Phillip. Knew how he scared all of them. He jabbed a thick finger against the boy's slate.

"These are scribbles, Mr Butler. How you can read them? I've no idea," he squinted. "And you've not even had the good sense to scribble them down correctly."

Two boys at the back of the classroom snickered.

"I'm sorry, sir." Grace could hear Phillip's voice wavering.

"To the front of the room, Mr Butler," the master barked. "This is simply not good enough."

Phillip's chair squeaked loudly as he got to his feet, trailing the master to the front of the schoolroom. Grace felt a lump in her throat. She tried to flash Phillip a look of solidarity but his eyes were on the floor, his mop of sandy hair hanging over his eyes and his bottom lip tucked between his teeth.

The master reached behind his desk for his cane. He brought it out with a flourish, waving it in front of the class for everyone to see. Phillip's chin trembled and Grace could tell that he was on the verge of tears. She willed him not to cry. Drake Matthews and the other nasty boys seated at the back of the classroom would never let him live it down.

"Hand out," the master said sharply. Phillip did so obediently without lifting his eyes from the floor. Out of the corner of her eye, Grace could see Drake grinning.

She gritted her teeth. Drake Matthews had always been nasty. In the two years she had known him, Grace had never heard him say a kind word to anybody. He and his friends had always been determined to poke fun at the kind and gentle boys; the likes of Phillip Butler.

Sometimes Grace heard her parents mumbling to each other about Drake's father.

*No good*, she had heard her father say once.

*Imagine the harm it's doing to that poor boy*, her mother had replied. When Grace had tried to pry out more information, her parents had told her off for eavesdropping and sent her back to bed. She had no thought of what her parents had been talking about, or exactly why Drake's father was no good. All she knew was that her life would be far more pleasant without Drake Matthews in it.

And so would Phillip's.

The cane came down with a sharp crack, making Phillip murmur in pain. Grace heard a snort of laughter from Drake and she whirled around sharply to glare at him. Drake ignored her.

"Mr Matthews?" the master snapped. "Do you wish to be next?"

"No, sir," Drake murmured, eyes falling back to the scrawls on his slate.

"Good." The master slid the cane back behind his desk. "Back to your seat, Mr Butler. I trust that will remind you to do better next time."

. . .

"IT'S NOT SO BAD," Grace said at lunchtime, peering down at the red streak that had appeared on Phillip's palm. "Does it hurt a lot?"

"A little." His voice was soft.

She flashed him a sympathetic smile. A few weeks ago, Grace had been the one standing at the front of the classroom to endure the sting of the school master's cane. She'd been late for school after oversleeping. She too had almost cried when the cane had come down on her hand. And the red welt on her palm had still been stinging when she'd crawled into bed that night.

She broke her slice of pound cake and held one half out to Phillip. "Here. Mama made it last night. It's delicious. It'll make your hand feel better, I promise."

Phillip's face lit up in a smile. "Thank you." They chewed in silence for a few moments. "It's good," he said finally.

Grace grinned. She'd known it would cheer him up.

Her eyes narrowed at the sight of Drake and his friends striding purposefully towards them. For a moment, she thought to pick up her lunch and run.

She had no desire to face Drake today. And she knew he would have horrible things to say about Phillip. But no. She would not be scared off by Drake Matthews. She was eight years old now. Old enough to stand up to mean boys just like him.

She fixed him with the fiercest glare she could muster. "Leave us alone."

Drake didn't even look at her. He reached down and shoved Phillip on the shoulder, making him drop the last of his cake.

"Hey!" cried Phillip.

Drake gave a snort of laughter. "You going to cry about that too, Butler?"

Phillip's cheeks flushed scarlet. "I did *not* cry."

The other boys howled with laughter.

"Leave him alone, Drake," Grace hissed. She got to her feet, grabbing Phillip's arm and pulling him up beside her. Suddenly, she didn't care about standing up to Drake Matthews. She just wanted to get as far away from him as possible. "Let's go, Phillip. They've got no idea what they're talking about."

As she strode off to the far side of the schoolyard, she could hear Drake's laughter echoing in her ears.

· · ·

GRACE HURRIED HOME from school with her woollen bonnet pulled low over her ears. Winter was approaching and the air was bitterly cold. Grace's fingers were stinging, even through her mittens, and she could feel her cheeks burning from the bracing wind. She leapt over an enormous puddle that had appeared in the middle of the street and hurried up the front path to her family's neat little home. Brightly coloured leaves blanketed the small front garden leaving the trees on either side of the gate bare black skeletons.

She let herself inside and was hit immediately by the warming aroma of her mother's cooking. Beef stew, Grace guessed. Her favourite. She took off her coat and bonnet, hanging them on the hook beside the front door and leaving her muddy boots in the hallway. She padded past the parlour in her stockinged feet, finding her mother, Veronica, in the kitchen.

Veronica looked up from the range and gave Grace a broad smile. "How was school, my darling?"

Grace leant up on her tiptoes to kiss her mother on the cheek. "Phillip got the cane again for writing his sums down all messy."

Veronica clicked her tongue. "That schoolmaster of yours is all too quick to get the cane out, isn't he?"

Grace nodded gravely. "Phillip didn't even deserve it. Drake's sums were much more messy."

Grace saw her mother flinch at the mention of Drake. Veronica made a noise in her throat but didn't respond. She went over to the table and pulled the cloth off a loaf of freshly baked bread sitting in its centre.

"Here," she told Grace. "You can cut us some slices to go with the stew." She handed her a knife. "Careful now. Keep your fingers away."

Grace nodded. She heard the same warning from her mother every time she helped slice the bread.

Veronica went back to the range, wiping her hands on the apron that was tied above her swollen belly. In three months, Grace would have a new brother or sister. She couldn't wait.

Concentrating hard, Grace began to slice through the bread, careful to make each slice even and mindful to keep her fingers out of the way.

"Is Papa home?" she asked.

"Not yet, my darling. It's Monday, remember?" Veronica kept her eyes on the stew. "Monday is Papa's busy day at the factory. But he'll be home soon." She flashed Grace a smile. "How about you set the table so we can eat as soon as Papa gets home?"

Grace nodded obediently. She cut the final slice of bread and then scampered to the kitchen cupboard to collect the bowls and spoons.

The front door creaked open as Grace was finishing setting the table. Her father, Llewellyn's, heavy footsteps thudded down the passage.

"Papa!" Grace ran out to meet him and he scooped her into his arms, ruffling her bright red hair. Her father was dressed in the neat black waistcoat and jacket he wore to work each day. She kissed him on the cheek, feeling his neatly trimmed beard tickle her skin.

"How was your day, Gracie?" he asked.

"It was all right." Llewellyn set her down and she grabbed his hand, tugging him into the kitchen. "Mama made beef stew for dinner."

Llewellyn smiled his crooked smile. "Beef stew. My favourite." He walked with Grace into the kitchen and then went to the range. He stood behind Veronica and wrapped his arms around her, pressing a kiss to her cheek and running a gentle hand over the swell of her belly. They murmured to each other in words Grace couldn't hear before Llewellyn took up his seat nearest the fire.

Grace perched on the edge of her chair, watching as her mother filled the bowls with steaming stew.

"How many today?" Veronica asked Llewellyn.

He stirred his soup, keeping his eyes on his bowl. "Three." His voice was low.

"Three what?" asked Grace.

Her father flashed her a bright smile. "We sent three brand new machines off to their new owners today."

"Oh." Grace stuck her spoon in her mouth. The factory in which her father worked seemed like such a mysterious place. They were always sending new machines off to their owners. What kind of machines were they, she always wondered. She had asked her father once, but his answer had been vague and confusing.

"Just machines," he had said. "To help people make things. Nothing you ought to bother yourself with."

THAT NIGHT, Grace lay in bed staring up at the dark beams of the roof. She couldn't stop thinking about Drake's snort of laughter when Phillip had been caned. Couldn't stop thinking about the way he and his friends had come after them in the schoolyard. Anger bubbled inside her. How pleasant the world would be without Drake Matthews in it. She sighed loudly and rolled over. She felt hours from sleep.

She could hear distant voices coming from the parlour downstairs. One of the voices belonged to her father. The other was unfamiliar. Who was the visitor, she wondered. Curious, Grace slipped out of bed and out onto the stairs. The voice belonged to George Howell, she realised, one of her father's good friends from church. She could hear the clink of bottles coming from the parlour. Could smell Papa's pipe smoke rising into the stairwell.

"Don't know how you do it, Llewellyn," Mr Howell was saying. "Certainly couldn't do it myself."

Grace's father was silent for several moments. "I'm only doing what the law dictates," he said finally.

"Of course. But still…"

"The trick to it is to keep them calm," Llewellyn continued. "That's the thing. Got to keep them calm at all costs. Got to remember it's not done for the spectacle of it, no matter how much certain other men might think otherwise."

Mr Howell hummed noncommittally. "Keep them calm," he repeated. "Must be easier said than done."

"At times," said Llewellyn. "Certainly."

Grace edged towards the landing, trying to catch more of the conversation. One of the stairs creaked loudly beneath her feet.

"Grace!" Her mother appeared suddenly at the bottom of the staircase. She planted her hands on her hips and frowned. "What are you doing out of bed?"

"I couldn't sleep."

Veronica strode up the stairs and grabbed Grace's hand. "That's no excuse to be roaming around the house. What have I told you about listening in on other people's conversations?"

"But, Mama, I—"

"Come on now," Veronica cut in. "Back to bed." She marched her daughter back up to her bedroom.

Grace scampered back to bed and pulled her blankets to her chin. "Mama?"

Veronica looked back at her from the hallway. "What is it, Grace?"

"What was Papa talking about? Why does he have to keep people calm?"

Veronica pressed her lips into a thin white line and at once Grace regretted asking the question. "He was talking about his work," her mother said finally. "Nothing more. Now go to sleep."

And Grace closed her eyes obediently, listening to her mother's footsteps as they disappeared rhythmically down the stairs.

## CHAPTER 2

*A* few days later, Grace was stepping through the school gates when Phillip came bounding up to her.

"Did you hear?" His blue eyes were shining with excitement. "Drake's father was arrested!"

Grace raised her eyebrows. "Arrested?" The word felt strangely thrilling on her tongue. She had never known anyone who had been arrested before. "Why? What did he do?"

"Thieving. My father heard he tried to steal the lead from the roof of the church at Saint Mary's. Papa says he's been carted off to Newgate."

Despite herself, Grace couldn't help a tiny smile. Drake's father was no good – her papa had said so himself. Surely if anyone deserved to be rotting in the cells at Newgate, it was him. Maybe that would teach Drake not to be so nasty.

Talk of Mr Matthews' arrest filtered through the classroom that morning. Everyone had their own version of the story.

"I heard the vicar was the one who caught him," said Lucy Dawson.

"My pa says he's going to get sent out," Johnny Harper announced.

"Silence!" the master barked, making Grace start. "If I hear another word, you'll all be working through lunchtime."

Grace said nothing but couldn't help her eyes from drifting to the empty desk at which Drake usually sat. Why had he not come to school today, she wondered. Did he know everyone would be speaking about his father's arrest? Did he not want to be on the receiving end of nasty comments such as the ones he so often hurled at Phillip?

On another of her eavesdropping expeditions one night, Grace had heard her parents talking about Drake and his family from her position on the stairs when she was unable to sleep.

"How he can even afford to send his child to school, I can't imagine," her mother had said. "You would imagine at his age, he should be peddling a cart somewhere to earn a crust."

"Thieving, if you ask me."

Veronica sighed. "Oh, Llewellyn. You don't know that for certain."

"I've come across enough men the likes of him in my lifetime. I know a crook when I see one."


A WEEK LATER, the news rippled through the class-room with even more nervous excitement. Drake's father was to face the hangman.

Grace stared at Drake's empty desk. He had not shown his face at school since the day of his father's arrest. Today, she felt none of the satisfac-tion she had felt on the day she had first heard about the arrest. As mean as Drake was, she couldn't help but feel sorry for him. She couldn't bear to imagine how it would feel if it were her father about to be hanged. How dreadful it would be to know someone you loved was going to have their life taken from them. She shook the thought away. Such a thing would never happen. Her father was far too good a man to ever face the hangman. That was something that happened to only the worst of criminals.

. . .

A WEEK LATER, Grace and Phillip were standing together outside the classroom, waiting for the bell to ring. Phillip nudged Grace suddenly.

"Look. Drake's here."

Grace turned to look. She was surprised to see him. A part of her had not expected Drake to return to school. He strode into the schoolyard with his hands dug into his pockets and a deep frown on his face. People shuffled away as he approached. Even the boys he usually spent his time with seemed hesitant to approach. As Drake neared the classroom, Grace found herself taking a step closer to Phillip.

In the two weeks during which Drake had been away, his eyes had hardened and his face seemed etched with a permanent scowl. The sight of him made Grace's stomach turn over with nerves. Although Drake was eight years old, the same age as her and Phillip, he seemed much older. Much tougher. Perhaps, Grace thought, that had come as a result of losing his father. Despite the fear Drake stirred up inside her, she couldn't shake off the thoughts of how hard the execution must have been for him. Had he watched, she found herself wondering. Or had he stayed tucked away at the home his father would never return to?

WITH THE QUESTION turning over and over in her mind, Grace found herself shooting curious glances at Drake throughout the day. Everyone was keeping their distance, she noticed. Even at lunchtime, Drake had been alone, striding off to the back of the yard to eat his food in silence. When the bell rang at the end of the school day, he shoved his chair back and strode out of the classroom without speaking to anybody. Grace sucked up her courage and hurried after him.

"Drake!" she called, her footsteps thumping behind him.

Drake whirled around. "What do you want?" he hissed.

Grace swallowed heavily at the sight of his dark, flashing eyes. "I just wanted to say…" Her voice came out tiny. "I'm sorry about your father. Really."

Drake's eyes narrowed as he looked her up and down. His lips parted and she could tell he was surprised she had approached him. But when he spoke, his voice was laced with bitterness.

"How can *you* be sorry?"

Grace frowned, taken aback by his cryptic response. But before she could answer, Drake was striding off, head down and hands shoved into his pockets.

Grace stared after him, a frown creasing the bridge of her nose. What did he mean by that? *How can* you *be sorry?*

"Grace!" She spun around to see Phillip jogging to catch up with her.

"Why were you talking to Drake?" he demanded.

Grace shrugged. An uncomfortable churning had sprung up in the bottom of her stomach. She wished she had stayed away from Drake just like everybody else. "I just wanted to tell him I was sorry. About his father." She shivered as a cold wind ripped across the schoolyard. She hurried out of the gate, Drake's bitter words echoing in her ears.

## CHAPTER 3

Grace trudged home from school, her boots crunching through the snow. She blew on her hands to warm them and tugged her bonnet down over her ears to protect them from the harsh wind. Though winter was long over, there was no warmth to the spring, the London sky still stubbornly grey.

Cold as it was, Grace was in no hurry to get home. Two months earlier, her mother had given birth to a baby girl who had not survived. The child had not uttered a single cry and they had buried her in the little graveyard at the back of Saint Mary's church. Ever since, a heaviness seemed to hang over the house. Her mother had stayed curled up in bed for more than a month, her eyes often swollen with tears shed. Grace had done her best to cheer her, cuddling up beside her in bed, bringing her gifts, and singing her favourite songs. She had even learned to make the pound cake her mother loved. Nothing had helped. When Grace had listened in on the murmured conversations between her parents, she had heard snatches of her mother's broken voice: *my fault, should have done more...* Though her baby sister had not lived a single day, her presence seemed to fill the place, constantly reminding them all of her loss. Their neat little terraced house that Grace had always hurried home to, was a place that now just made her sad.

When Grace got to the house, she froze. A streak of bright red paint was splashed across the front door. She stared, the muscles in her shoulders tightening. The vividness of the paint reminded her of blood and for a moment she was afraid to approach. Finally, she hurried up the front steps and let herself inside, keeping her eyes on her feet to avoid looking at the paint.

"Mama?" she called.

"In here, my darling."

Grace was glad to hear Veronica's voice coming from the kitchen rather than the bedroom. She hurried down the passage without bothering to remove her coat or snowy boots. She found her mother at the kitchen table, slowly peeling a pile of potatoes.

Grace rushed to her side and flung her arms around her shoulders. It was a rare occasion to find her mother out of bed these days.

"How was school?" Veronica's smile was forced.

"Why is there red paint on the door?" Grace asked worriedly.

Something flickered across her mother's eyes and Grace could tell Veronica had no idea it was there.

"Red paint?" she repeated thinly.

"Yes. All over the door."

Veronica gave another strained smile but she kept her eyes on the potatoes without looking at Grace. "Someone has had an accident perhaps," she said meekly. "Had a spill."

"A spill?" Grace repeated. "No, Mama, this wasn't a spill. It was like—"

Veronica got to her feet quickly, her chair squealing against the flagstones as she stood up. She thumped the kettle onto the stove.

"I'll make you some tea, love," she said. "It's

dreadfully cold out there. Now take your boots off before you catch a chill."

THE NEXT MORNING, the red paint was gone. Grace had heard her father out in the street the previous night, painting over it with a thick layer of green. But as Grace stepped out of the house on her way to school the next morning, she still imagined she could see a crimson shadow where the red stripe had been. She quickly pulled her eyes away.

Walking beside her, Llewellyn gave her hand a firm squeeze. "It's all right, Gracie. It's nothing to worry yourself over."

Grace was glad her father had decided to walk her to school that day. "Mama said someone had an accident. A spill."

He nodded. "That's right. Nothing to worry yourself over." His words sounded rehearsed. Grace hadn't believed her mother and she did not believe her father either. But she didn't want to speak of it any more.

They made their way through the narrow streets towards the school. Grace clung tightly to her father's hand as they skirted the puddles among the cobbles. She could see the sharp spires of the church poking through the thick bank of cloud.

She thought of Drake Matthews' father, hanged for stealing lead from the church roof.

They turned the corner and found a man and a young child walking towards them. The man grabbed the boy's hand and tugged him onto the other side of the street. He glared at Llewellyn.

"Scum," the man hissed.

Grace looked up at her father, bewildered. But he had not seemed to notice.

"Papa?"

He gave her a smile that looked too broad. "Yes, love?"

"Was that man talking to you?"

"Of course not," he said hurriedly. "I've no idea who he is."

Grace glanced back over her shoulder, trying to catch another glimpse of the man and the boy. But when she looked back, they had disappeared.

She and her father stopped outside the school gates and Llewellyn let go of her hand. He bent to kiss her, his beard tickling her cheek. "Have a good day, Grace."

She nodded. Just before she darted off, Llewellyn grabbed her hand, tugging her back to him. He looked at her squarely. "You're not to worry about any of this," he said, his big hands wrapped around her shoulders. "You're not to worry about the paint or the people in the street."

Grace swallowed. "What about Mama?"

Llewellyn smiled gently. "You're not to worry about Mama either. She's going to be just fine. We all are." He kissed her again. "Now off you go. Have a good day."

Grace drifted towards her classroom, deep in thought. She had no doubt the man in the street had been speaking to her father.

*Scum*, he had said. Grace didn't understand. Her father was the kindest man she had ever known. How could anyone hurl insults at him as he walked down the street? And why would someone throw red paint all over their door?

"It's probably like your ma said," Phillip told her when she shared her concerns with him at lunchtime. "Maybe someone had a spill."

Grace nodded. But she couldn't manage to convince herself.

VERONICA DILLINGHAM WAS glad when silence fell over the house. She curled up in bed, pulling her blankets up over her head. Doing so felt as though she could make the world around her disappear, if only for a few moments.

But even with the blankets over her head and darkness pressing down on her, Veronica couldn't still her thoughts. Every time she closed her eyes, she could see the violent stripe of red paint splashed across their front door.

It was far from a rare occurrence. She could vividly remember the first time it had happened. She and Llewellyn had been married less than a month. They had returned from an evening at the music hall to find the door of their house branded in red. At first she had not understood what it was or who had done it. But as she watched her new husband's shoulder sink, she realised. This was his penance, she had learned then. This was the price he had to pay for the way he spent his days.

Veronica had known from the beginning, of course, the way Llewellyn earned a living. He had told her it all in a shy half voice early in their courtship, as though he was confessing to a crime. She could tell even then that there was guilt in him because of it. But the fact remained that his job paid well. Well enough to keep him and his family fed and warm and longing for nothing. Marrying Llewellyn Dillingham would ensure she had a good life. Besides, Veronica loved him dearly. And so she had chosen to look past the way he earned his money and had become his wife despite it.

"It's not important to me," she remembered telling him on the day he had asked for her hand. "I know what a kind and decent man you are. And that's all that matters."

When she had uttered those words, Veronica had believed them wholeheartedly. But as the years had rolled by, she had begun to see her naivety. The red paint on the door. The abuse hurled in the street. The looks given to them by strangers, the comments whispered behind hands. Veronica took them all as personally as if they were directed solely at her. And with each passing day, month, year, they became harder to shake off.

Each day, she felt as though a heaviness were pressing down upon her, a darkness she could not crawl out from beneath. She knew Llewellyn held himself responsible for her melancholy, and for his sake she had tried to pull herself out of it. But she felt utterly unable. She longed to be the carefree girl she had once been; the girl whose smiles were genuine and whose laughter was not strained.

Things had only become worse after she had held her lost baby girl in her arms; that poor tiny child who had never cried. Never taken a breath. Veronica had wondered if her melancholy had been to blame. Had her child somehow sensed the cruel nature of the world she was about to enter? It was a thought she could not afford to follow far.

Veronica had tried to gather herself after the death of the baby. She knew Grace needed her and that she missed her mother's laughter and their easy chatter around the supper table. The side table in her bedroom was cluttered with drawings and the single daisies in vases that Grace had brought her in an attempt to lift her spirits.

"I made vegetable soup, Mama," she would announce proudly. Or, "I need you to help me with the bread."

And around her daughter, Veronica had felt flickers of happiness and seen fleeting glimpses of a life not overshadowed by sadness. But the paint on the door yesterday had sent her crumbling back to the dark place she had been in on the day she had buried her baby. This morning she had been unable to leave her bed.

And now Grace was starting to ask questions. Veronica had always known this day was coming. And a part of her had been dreading it since the moment Grace was born. She had hoped to keep the truth hidden for a few more years at least, but she was coming to see that was not an option. Grace was far too sharp-witted for that.

Veronica cringed when she thought of the excuse she'd garbled out the night before. *Someone has had an accident perhaps...*

Little wonder Grace had looked back at her with disbelief in her eyes.

Veronica knew she couldn't continue to keep the truth from her daughter. Grace deserved far better than that. But what would it do to her when she learned what her father really was?

She let out an enormous sigh, hugging her knees to her chest beneath the blankets. Perhaps she was worried for no good reason. Grace had always idolised Llewellyn. Perhaps she would simply absorb this new information as just another part of who her father was. Continue to look up to him, respect him, adore him. And at eight years old, would she even understand the magnitude of just what her father did?

Either way, Veronica knew they had to tell

Grace the truth before she learned it from one of those awful boys at school.

She hated that her daughter might be forced to spend her days sitting across the classroom from Roger Matthews' son. She had little doubt Drake was as vile and crooked as his father had been. She was glad Grace had a friend in little Phillip Butler, though she doubted the boy would be much good when it came to standing up to bullies the likes of Drake. Phillip had always been shy and timid; much more than Grace herself.

One day soon, Veronica told herself, she would sit Grace down and tell her everything. She only prayed her daughter would understand.

WHEN THE BELL rang that afternoon, Grace felt a familiar sense of dread pressing down on her shoulders. What state would her mother be in when she got home this afternoon? Grace knew she had been lucky to find Veronica up and about the previous day. She knew she would likely not be so lucky today.

Once, Grace remembered, Veronica had been so full of life. Her blue eyes had sparkled and the house was always filled with her laughter. How Grace missed her. How she wished things could go back to the way they had been before her mother's laughter had faded away. Before they had buried her tiny sister in the graveyard behind Saint Mary's.

Nor could she bear to go home and see another angry red stripe of paint on their door. Was it possible the man insulting her father that morning had had something to do with the paint? Grace's thoughts were knocking together. Nothing made sense anymore. She felt suddenly close to tears.

She trudged towards the school gates, biting her lip to keep herself from crying. She felt a sudden, violent shove in the back. She pitched forward, stumbling onto her knees. She scrambled back to her feet, laughter echoing in her ears. She spun around, coming face to face with three of the older boys from her class. Her heart began to pound.

"How many men did your father kill this week, Dillingham?" spat one.

Grace stared up at him with wide eyes. "What?"

One of the boys stepped closer, his breath hot against her cheek. "Don't you know your papa is a murderer?"

Grace's stomach turned over. Her father a murderer? She had never heard anything so foolish – and yet she couldn't help the stab of dread inside her.

"He is not," she managed, but her voice was so tiny she was sure none of them had heard her. "My father never killed anyone."

One of the boys stepped close. "Liar."

Grace blinked away her tears. "I'm not lying."

One of the other boys broke into a wild peal of laughter. "She doesn't know!" he cackled. "She doesn't know how many men her father's sent down to hell!"

The boys began to howl with laughter as though they had never heard anything so amusing in their entire lives.

Grace broke into a sudden run, tearing through the gates of the schoolyard. She sloughed through the mud on the side of the road, passing the place where the man had insulted her father that morning. She splashed through a puddle, dirty water spraying up her stockings and soaking through the top of her shoes. By the time she got home, tears were flooding down her cheeks and her skirts were splattered with mud. She let herself inside, stopping abruptly. She recognised the voice of their vicar coming from the kitchen. She couldn't make out his words.

"Is that you, Grace?" her mother called.

Grace hurriedly wiped her eyes. She didn't want the vicar to see her crying. With her head down, she crept into the kitchen. Her mother and father were sitting at the table with the vicar, a teapot in the middle of the table and steaming cups in front of each of them.

"Come and sit down, love," said Llewellyn. "Have some tea to warm yourself—" He stopped abruptly when he caught sight of her swollen red eyes.

"Whatever has happened, my darling?" asked Veronica. Grace rushed to her mother, no longer caring about hiding her tears. She buried her head in Veronica's shoulder. Felt her mother's arm wrap around her. Grace clung tighter to her. It had been far too long since her mother had held her like this. She never wanted to let go.

Finally, her mother eased her out of the embrace. "What's happened?" she asked again, tucking a strand of hair behind Grace's ear.

Grace sniffed, wiping her eyes with the back of her hand. "The boys at school," she began. "They said…" She broke down into another sudden rush of tears. How could she put into words the dreadful things those boys had said? How could she repeat it?

*Murderer.*

"Grace?" her father spoke up. "What did they say?"

Grace turned to look at him. Llewellyn and the vicar were both peering down at her with concern in their eyes. Grace sucked in her breath. "They said bad things about you, Papa. They said... they said you killed people. They said you're a murderer. And that you sent lots of men down to hell." She coughed down her tears, throwing herself into her mother's arms again.

For several moments, no one spoke. Grace's faint sobbing sounded loud in the stillness. The vicar's chair creaked noisily.

"Your father is a good man, Grace," he told her. "He is a good man carrying out the duties of his office. He helps keep many people safe. Make sure you always remember that."

Grace looked over her mother's shoulder at the vicar.

"Promise me you will always remember that." He peered at her with his intense grey eyes; eyes that matched his thinning hair. His round cheeks were pink. Though Grace knew the vicar as a jolly man full of smiles, today his face was stern and serious.

She nodded tearfully. "I promise."

"Good girl." The vicar tossed back the last of his tea and got to his feet. "Thank you for the tea, Mrs Dillingham." He turned to Llewellyn. "If there's anything else you need, you know where to find me."

Llewellyn nodded. "Thank you, Father."

The vicar reached over and squeezed his shoulder. "I can see myself out." His footsteps echoed down the hallway, a burst of cold air creeping into the house as he opened the front door and stepped out into the street.

Llewellyn patted the chair left empty by the vicar. "Here, Gracie. Come and sit by me."

Grace climbed onto the chair while her mother filled a cup from the teapot and handed it to her. She wrapped her hands around the cup, warmth seeping into her frozen fingers. She took a mouthful of tea, feeling it begin to settle her slightly. The vicar had said her father was a good man and the vicar wouldn't lie. Those boys were wrong about her father. They had to be. After a moment, she dared to look up at her parents.

"Why would the boys say those things?" she asked. "Why would they say you killed people?"

Her father ran a hand through his thick sandy hair. Grace saw a wordless glance pass between her parents. Veronica gave the faintest of nods. Then Llewellyn turned back to face her.

"It's my job, Gracie," he said gently.

She frowned. "What? I don't understand. Killing people is your job?"

Llewellyn sighed and for a moment his eyes flickered back to Veronica but then he reached out and took Grace's hand.

"When people do bad things," he began carefully, "the law says they are to be put to death. Hanged."

Grace looked up at Llewellyn. "Like Drake's father?"

He nodded. "That's right. Just like Drake's father. And it's my job to put those people to death."

Grace chewed her lip, the pieces beginning to fall into a place.

"You mean you're a hangman?" Her parents had never permitted her to watch a hanging but she had heard stories about them from many of her friends at school. Even Phillip had once watched a man get put to death. He had gone to the gallows outside Newgate to watch William Calcraft hang a man convicted of murder. He had told her all about the drawn-out execution; the way the man had still been alive when he had fallen to the end of the rope. The way Calcraft had yanked on his legs in order to break the man's neck. And the way the crowd had cheered. At the thought of her father doing such things, her throat tightened, her tears threatening to return.

"Yes, Grace," Llewellyn said, his voice low. "That's what I do."

"Do you ever pull on their legs to make them die?" she asked. "Like William Calcraft?"

"Grace!" Her mother looked aghast. "Wherever did you hear that?"

But Llewelyn just reached over and pressed a soft hand to his daughter's shoulder. "No, Grace," he said, his voice gentle. "I never do that. I'm always very careful. I make sure they don't suffer."

Grace sniffed. So it was true. Her father had killed other men. But surely this did not make him a murderer? Did it?

"But why, Papa?" she asked. "Why do you have to kill them at all?"

Llewellyn stroked her hair. "I'm just carrying

out the sentences of the courts, Grace. Those that are put to death are bad people. They're thieves. Violent people. Sometimes they've even killed people themselves."

"Your father is doing his country a good service," Veronica spoke up. "You ought to be proud of him."

Grace peered up at Llewellyn who ventured a small smile. After a moment, she gave a small nod.

"Is that why someone put red paint on our door?" she asked finally.

"Yes, love," Llewellyn said. "Maybe someone was angry because I had to hang someone they cared about."

"But you were only doing your job," Grace said. "You were only doing what the courts said you were to do."

"That's right." Llewellyn leaned over and kissed the side of her head. "I'm glad you understand, my love."

Grace slid from her chair and wrapped her arms around her father. She could feel his heart beating rapidly beside her own.

## CHAPTER 4

*W*hen Grace stepped out of the house the next morning she saw how a fresh bloom of red paint had been hurled across their front door. Today, instead of putting her head down and avoiding looking at it, she stood for a moment with her eyes fixed to its brightness; stark against the bleakness of the morning.

She thought of her father's words: *Maybe someone was angry because I was asked to hang someone they cared about.*

The thought made her shiver. Who had come to her door in the night? Thieves? Murderers? Or perhaps just a wife or daughter mourning a man they loved?

Though the thought was an uncomfortable one, the sight of the paint didn't scare her the way it had last time. At least now she understood.

The night before, she had lain awake for a long time, thinking about all her parents had told her. So her father did not work at a factory or send machines to their new owners. When her father went to work each day in his neat black suit, it was to send men to their death. Her father had killed people just like the boys in her class had said. But Grace knew that did not make him a murderer. He was only doing as the courts told him to. Murderers were bad people. And her father was the best man she had ever known.

Grace had repeated those words to herself over and over as she'd waited for sleep to pull her down. The reality of what her father did had rattled her, but she was glad her parents had told her the truth.

"GET MY LITTLE GIFT THIS MORNING?" Drake asked as Grace stepped through the school gates.

Grace stopped walking. She gritted her teeth. "You were the one who put the paint on our door."

Despite herself, the thought chilled her. How did Drake know where her family lived? Had he followed her home from school one day? And had he come out to their house in the night all alone? Or did he have a mother, brothers, sisters, who had helped deface the house?

At the sight of Grace's discomfort, the corner of Drake's lips turned up. He said nothing, but his dark eyes seemed to bore into her. Grace was glad to see Phillip jogging across the yard towards them.

He took her arm gently. "Come on. Let's go." He flashed Drake an angry glance, before turning away hurriedly.

"Your father's going to burn in hell," Drake called after them.

Grace stopped walking and spun around to face him. "What did you say?"

Drake grinned. "You heard me." The dark smiled disappeared suddenly and he took a step towards her. "He killed my father. And my father was innocent." His eyes flashed. "So that murdering father of yours is going to burn in hell."

Grace felt her eyes fill with sudden tears. She had had no idea that her father had been the one to send Roger Matthews to his death. She stared up at Drake. Ought she to tell him that she was sorry? No, she decided. She wasn't sorry. Her father only did as the courts told him to. He would not burn in hell for that. And she would not apologise for her father doing what was right.

Before she could speak, Phillip lurched at Drake, shoving him hard in the chest. Drake stumbled backwards in surprise. Grace's eyes widened. She had never seen Phillip act so aggressively before.

"Leave her alone," he hissed.

Drake chuckled. "Or what? You going to fight me, Butler? Just try it."

Phillip charged at him suddenly. Drake swung a wild fist, catching Phillip beneath his eye. He stumbled to his knees. Grace heard a scream escape her. She rushed to Phillip's side.

"Are you all right?" she asked breathlessly.

Phillip managed a nod, although he had a hand clamped to his cheek. Grace heard Drake chuckling as he disappeared towards the classroom.

"What are you doing?" she asked Phillip. "Why would you fight Drake?"

Phillip stayed planted on the ground, water soaking through his trousers. "Because he can't say things like that to you. It's awful." His eyes were hard and angry as he stared in the direction Drake had disappeared. Grace felt a warmth in her chest that Phillip might do such a thing on her behalf.

For a moment she sat motionless beside him. "My papa is a hangman."

Phillip didn't speak at once. "Like William Calcraft?" he said finally.

Grace nodded. "Yes. But he doesn't do awful things like William Calcraft. He makes sure people don't suffer when they die." The words felt strange on her tongue. It was the first time she had spoken aloud about what her father did. She glanced at Phillip. A part of her was nervous, she realised. How would her friend react when he learned this about her family?

"Did he kill Drake's father?" he asked.

Grace shrugged. "I don't know."

Phillip stared across the yard for a moment, watching Drake talking with the other boys. "Even if he did, everyone knows Drake's father deserved it."

Grace chewed her lip. "You don't mind? What my father does?"

Phillip frowned. "Why would I mind?"

Grace felt her shoulders sink in relief. "I don't know. I just thought maybe…" She trailed off. She held out her hand to help Phillip to his feet.

"Thank you for standing up to Drake," she said. "That was very brave."

Phillip managed a small smile. The skin beneath his eye had already turned bright red. "Don't listen to anything Drake says," he told her. "Everyone knows he's no good."

"DID YOU HANG DRAKE'S FATHER?" Grace asked Llewellyn that night. They were sitting in front of the fire in the parlour; Llewellyn stretched out in his favourite armchair, while Grace sat beside the hearth with her sewing in her lap. Veronica had disappeared to her bedroom the moment supper was finished.

Llewellyn looked up from the bottle of ale in his hand. "Who told you that?"

Grace picked at the hem of the skirt she was mending. "Drake. He and Phillip got into a fight. He said…" She faded out. She would not repeat the dreadful things Drake Matthews had said about her father.

Llewellyn let out a long sigh. He put down his bottle. "I did hang him, Gracie. But it was my job. I was—"

"Doing what the courts said," Grace finished.

Her father nodded. "That's right." He reached down to ruffle her hair.

Grace stared into the fire. Already, she regretted starting the conversation. "Drake said his father was innocent."

"Did he now?" Llewellyn didn't look at her.

"Is that what you think too?"

He ran a finger down the side of the bottle. "Roger Matthews was found at the bottom of the church tower with a ladder and pile of lead. There was no question about him being guilty."

"So he did it?" Grace chewed her lip.

Llewellyn took another long sip. "I'll tell you something, Gracie, but you're not to repeat it." His voice was suddenly dark and serious. "There are certain things that are not to be shared, do you understand?"

She nodded, eyes wide.

"Before the men and women are put to death, they're given the chance to speak with a priest," Llewellyn began. "Given the chance to confess their crimes. I was there when the priest came for Drake's father on the morning he was hanged. He confessed to the theft of the lead and plenty of other things besides. He wanted to go to his death with a clear conscience."

47

Grace frowned. "So why did Drake say he was innocent?"

"Maybe that's what he needed to believe," her father said gently. "Maybe it was easier for him that way."

Grace nodded slowly. Despite herself, she couldn't help a small pang of pity for Drake. Then she thought of the way he had swung his fist at Phillip and the pity evaporated.

"What happened next?" she dared to ask. "After Mr Matthews spoke to the priest?" Her heartbeat began to speed as she asked the question. She knew well what had happened next; her father had hanged him. But she needed to hear the words from his lips. She knew her father would tell her the truth. And knowing what had really happened somehow made it easier to stand up and look Drake in the eye.

Llewellyn shifted uncomfortably in his chair and for a moment Grace thought he was not going to speak. But then, he said, "Well, then he was led to the gallows. A small crowd was watching."

"Did the crowd know it was you?" Grace asked. "Who hanged him?"

Llewellyn turned his bottle around in his hands. "Some of them, perhaps. I always wear a hood so I can't be recognised. But I have friends who know what I do."

*And some enemies*, Grace thought sadly, thinking of the paint splashed across their front door.

"Did you have to pull on Mr Matthews' legs?" Grace asked. "Like William Calcraft has to do?"

"No, Grace. I've told you that before." The fire popped noisily. "Mr Matthews' death was very quick. And he was very calm." He looked down at her, giving her a ghost of a smile. "That's the trick, you see. To always keep them calm. It's what I always strive to do." He sat back in his chair and brought the bottle to his lips again. When he spoke again, his voice was low, and almost to himself he said, "Always keep them calm."

* * *

*ALWAYS KEEP THEM CALM.*

How many times had Veronica heard her husband say that over the years? She buried her head under the pillow, trying to block out the voices that were drifting up from the parlour.

She had expected to feel a small sense of achievement when she and Llewellyn finally told their daughter the truth. But all she felt was a deep ache.

Thanks to their hesitance to speak up, what Veronica had dreaded most had come to pass: Grace had learned the truth about her father from those awful boys at school. The moment she had seen her daughter rush into the kitchen with red, swollen eyes, she had known they were too late.

She tried to console herself with the knowledge that Grace was strong. Far stronger than her mother, Veronica thought wryly. She had taken the truth in her stride. But now her curiosity had her asking questions.

Veronica couldn't blame her, of course, but she couldn't push away the pain inside her. A pain that came from the knowledge that now so many of their family conversations would be taken up with talk from the gallows.

Llewellyn had always spoken a lot of his work; Veronica knew it was his way of coping with the guilt. And for that reason, she had always forced herself to listen, to respond, and to offer as much support as she could muster.

But back when Grace had believed her father a mere factory worker, they'd had a reprieve from such discussions whenever their daughter was around. At least at the supper table there could be no talk of who had been put to death or which prisoners had confessed. There could be no talk about the importance of *always keeping them calm.*

Now Veronica knew she would have no such luxury. The truth of who her husband was had just become even more inescapable.

## CHAPTER 5

Grace wrapped her cloak around herself tightly and stared down at the grave. There was her mother's name, almost hidden by the ice glittering on the headstone. Snow drifted down from a colourless sky, settling silently in the churchyard. It had been a year since Veronica had passed – and almost five years since they had buried her baby daughter in this very same cemetery.

Grace shuffled backwards and stood with her shoulder pressed against her father's arm. Llewellyn reached an arm around her and squeezed.

"I miss her, Papa," Grace said through the tears that were tightening her throat.

Llewellyn nodded but didn't speak. Grace didn't need him to. She knew how intensely her father missed his wife.

Llewellyn had not been the same since Veronica's death. He barely spoke a word these days and spent most evenings staring into a bottle of whisky. Grace supposed she hadn't been the same either. Still, how could either of them be, after all that had happened? How were they supposed to just carry on with their lives?

Veronica's melancholy had worsened over the years, and in the months before her death, she had barely left her bed. Grace had taken over the running of the house; the hours after she came home from school had been filled with cooking and cleaning and trying to coax her mother down to the supper table. Each morning, she had risen before dawn to light the fires and ensure her father had a cup of tea and a warm breakfast before heading off to Stepney Prison.

A year earlier, just after Christmas, Veronica had emerged from her bedroom to join Grace and Llewellyn by the fire in the parlour. She had said almost nothing but her mere presence had gone a long way towards convincing Grace that one day soon, Veronica would be all right. Convince her that her warm and bubbly mother would somehow find her way back to them.

The next morning, Veronica had left her bed again. She had pulled on her cloak and boots and walked out of the house without so much as a word to Grace, who was preparing breakfast in the kitchen. She strode out into the street and threw herself under the wheels of the first carriage to pass.

Sometimes, Grace was angry at her mother for leaving them. Sometimes, she blamed herself – tried to think of what else she might have done to stop her mother from feeling the way she had.

Mostly, she was just sad.

It hadn't just been the loss of the baby that had caused Veronica's grief, Grace knew well. Things had not been easy since word had spread about her father's job. At least once a month they would come home to red paint splattered across the front door. And the jibes in the street had become so commonplace that Grace had learnt to ignore them. But she knew her mother had found it difficult. While many of their friends and acquaintances were kind and understanding of Llewellyn's position, many people despised him for it. Many people saw him as little more than a cold-blooded killer. People would hurl abuse at Llewellyn when they saw him in the street. Would whisper behind their hands in the churchyard, out of earshot of the vicar.

On more than one occasion, Veronica had pressed Llewellyn to leave the job. Each time he had refused. The pay was excellent, he had argued; far more than he would earn working gruelling hours in a factory. Their house had not come cheap, he had told her. And he wanted nothing more than to provide a good life for his family. He would not have them living in some filthy Whitechapel tenement. But in the end, that need for a good income had played such an enormous role in Veronica's death.

Grace wondered if these were the thoughts her father was trying to drown each time he lost himself in a bottle of whisky. Would things have been different if he had stepped away from the gallows and taken a job at a factory? Would Veronica still be alive if they were huddled together in a filthy Whitechapel tenement?

Grace cast one last look at her mother's headstone, then tugged on Llewellyn's arm. "Let's go, Papa. It's ever so cold."

Llewellyn nodded wordlessly, walking towards the churchyard gate with a hand pressed to Grace's shoulder. They hurried back towards home, the snow thickening as they walked. It billowed around the streetlamps, casting a hazy orange glow over the dusk.

Grace stepped inside and kicked off her boots, hurrying into the parlour to restoke the fire. Llewellyn appeared behind her. He took the half-drunk whisky bottle from the side table and pulled out the cork. He took a long mouthful.

Grace eyed the bottle warily. "Sit down, Papa. Rest. I'll make us some supper."

Llewellyn sank into his favourite armchair, not relinquishing his grip on the bottle.

Grace went to the kitchen and placed the soup on the range to heat. She had become adept at cooking, though making the same meals her mother had once prepared filled her with a dull ache. Each time the house filled with the smell of baking bread or roasting meat, she would remember sitting at the kitchen table, watching her mother flit around the kitchen. Would hear her mother's words as she handed Grace the bread knife:

*Careful now. Keep your fingers away.*

Now thirteen, Grace had finished her schooling for which she was glad. Keeping house each evening after she returned from her lessons had been exhausting. Plus, not going to school meant she did not need to see Drake Matthews every day. And that was certainly something to be grateful for.

The soup began to bubble and she spooned it carefully into two bowls. She called Llewellyn into the kitchen.

They ate wordlessly, the silence punctuated by the tapping of their spoons against the side of their bowls and the gentle crackling of the fire. Grace missed the days when her father had chatted to her while they ate their supper. Since Veronica's death, he had become quiet and withdrawn.

When he pushed his empty bowl aside and said, "Thank you, Gracie," the sound of his voice made her start.

Llewellyn took his coat from the hook beside the door and slipped it over his broad shoulders.

Grace frowned. "Where are you going, Papa?"

"Out." He didn't look at her.

She got to her feet and peered out the window. The snow was still falling heavily, the street an eerie white in the glow of the street lamps.

"It's still snowing, Papa. It's not a good night to be outside."

He gave a strained smile. "I'll be just fine. Don't you worry."

Grace gripped the back of her chair. "Are you going to the tavern again?"

Llewellyn said nothing but Grace didn't need the confirmation. Whenever Llewellyn left the house these days, it was either to work at Stepney Prison or to go to the taverns and gambling halls. Sometimes when he came home in his cups, he'd tell Grace about the men in the bars who congratulated him on the important work he was doing. Men would buy him drinks all night, he would boast.

"One man even called me a hero," he told her once. "Said I was cleansing the earth of all the villains." He chuckled loudly. "Can you believe that, Gracie? Me, a hero!"

Grace understood. She had seen first-hand how much abuse her father was forced to withstand.

And she knew well of the guilt he carried over her mother's death. To be called a hero must have eased that guilt and self-loathing, even for a moment. But she didn't want her father in the taverns tonight. After visiting Veronica's grave, she missed her mother more than usual. She needed her father's company – even if they were to just sit in the parlour in silence. Tonight it would be enough just to have him near.

"Please don't go out tonight, Papa," Grace begged. She looked up at him pleadingly. "Please stay here with me."

Llewellyn's shoulders slumped. "Well," he said, "I suppose I could stay. I—"

"It's all right," Grace said quickly. As much as she wanted her father's company, she did not want to deprive him of his much-needed relaxation. If going out to the taverns and being called a hero would make him feel better, then she would not stand in his way. "You go. I'm going to go to bed anyway. I'm ever so tired."

Llewellyn rubbed his beard. "Are you sure?"

Grace forced a smile. "Of course. I'll see you in the morning."

She stood up on her tiptoes and kissed her father's cheek.

.  .  .

THE HOUSE FELT cold and empty after her father had left. Grace washed their supper dishes and then made her way wearily up to bed. Maybe an early night would do her good.

But exhausted as she was, her mind refused to still and she lay on her back staring up into the blackness. She could hear muted voices coming from the street outside their house.

Troublemakers, she wondered. Would she wake to another dose of red paint across their front door?

The police patrolled this street regularly now and had done so ever since a brick had been put through the window one night. Grace was sure it had come from someone like Drake who believed his executed father to be innocent.

The voices disappeared, leaving a thick, weighty silence. Grace rolled onto her side and closed her eyes. But it was not until she heard her father stumble drunkenly home several hours later that she was finally able to sleep.

.  .  .

A FEW WEEKS LATER, Grace was walking with Phillip along the riverbank. Though the air was still bitterly cold, the day was bright; the sun streaming down upon the city, although it brought little warmth.

They walked close together on the riverbank, their shoulders pressing against each other's. Grace missed seeing Phillip every day at school but they visited each other as often as they could. He was a source of constant comfort to her; had been endlessly supportive as she'd navigated her mother's death.

"Drake's not at school anymore," Phillip told her as they walked. "He stopped coming a few weeks ago."

Grace nodded. She wasn't surprised. In truth, she was surprised Drake had attended classes for as long as he had. In the five years of her schooling, she couldn't remember him ever showing an interest in learning anything. Couldn't remember him showing an interest in anything except bullying the other students. She was glad Phillip no longer had to see him each day.

"Must be much more pleasant without him," she said.

Phillip chuckled. "Much more pleasant."

"What do you imagine he'll do?" Grace asked. "Take a job in a factory?"

Phillip let out his breath. "Honest work? I'm sorry to say, I can't see that happening. I'm sure he's already turned to crime."

Grace murmured noncommittally. She suspected Phillip was right.

"How's your father?" he asked, peering down at her. Over the past few years, he had grown tall and slender and now towered over Grace.

She dug her hands into the pockets of her coat. "I'm worried about him," she admitted. "He's off to the tavern several nights a week. And I'm sure he's gambling."

Phillip flashed her a sympathetic smile. "Maybe that's what he needs to take his mind off things."

Grace nodded. She had often wondered how heavily Llewellyn's job weighed on his mind. She knew, of course, that he carried great guilt over her mother's death. But did he also carry guilt over the lives he took in the name of duty?

"Do you think my father a good man?" she heard herself ask. The words had fallen out without her having any thought of it.

Phillip frowned at her slightly. "Do you really need to ask that?"

Grace let out her breath, hit with a sudden pang of guilt. No, she thought. She didn't need to ask that. She had always known her father to be the best of men. The past year had just been especially difficult for him. It had been for both of them.

"No," she said. "I don't. I know my father is a good man. I know he only does the things he does out of duty." And as for the drunkenness and the gambling, well they were just his way of coping with a tragic loss. Who would not allow him that?

She would buy him a treat, she decided suddenly. They were close to Leadenhall Market – she would buy him some of the raisin cake he was so fond of.

"Will you walk me to the market?" she asked. "I'd like to buy some cake for him."

Phillip smiled. "I'm sure he'll appreciate that."

They turned away from the riverbank and wove through the streets of Billingsgate, Grace's hand tucked neatly into the crook of Phillip's arm. The streets outside the market were swarming with shoppers. Everyone had taken advantage of the fine weather, it seemed.

When they reached the entrance to the market, Grace slid her hand free. "No need to come in with me," she said. "It looks dreadfully busy." She flashed him a smile. "Thank you for a lovely afternoon. Will I see you again soon?" How she missed seeing him every day at school.

Phillip grinned. "Of course. We can go to the park next week if you like. If the sun's out, of course."

Grace returned his smile. "I'd like that very much."

She waved goodbye to Phillip and headed into the market, her hand wrapped tightly around the coin pouch in her pocket.

The market hall was noisy; filled with the shouts of vendors, and a cacophony of voices and laughter. She followed the rich aroma of warm bread until she found the bakery.

A cluster of people was gathered around the baker's stall, and Grace stood on her tiptoes to peer at the food.

There were two raisin cakes left at the back of the table. She smiled to herself as she dug into her pocket for her coins, thinking of the way her father's face would light up when he saw them.

Suddenly, her arm was ripped backwards, the coins spilling to the floor. Grace cried out in shock and whirled around, coming face to face with Drake Matthews. It had been almost a year since she had seen him. In that time he had grown impossibly tall and broad-shoulders, a dark shadow of hair on his upper lip. He looked far older than thirteen. He stared at Grace with hatred in his eyes. The sight of him made her stomach turn over in dread. She had little doubt that Phillip was right about Drake turning to crime.

"What do you want, Drake?" she asked, forcing herself to stay calm. There were plenty of people around. Surely he wouldn't do anything to harm her in such a busy place.

"How's your killer of a father doing?" he asked bitterly.

Grace straightened her shoulders. She would not let herself be scared by Drake. Nor would she let him sway her into believing Llewellyn was anything but utterly decent. Forcing herself to stay calm, she bent to pick up her fallen coins, hardly daring to take her eyes from Drake.

"My father is a good man," she said evenly. "The only people he has ever put to death are those who were sent to the gallows by the courts."

Drake laughed coldly. "A good man? Is that what you call it? My father was innocent. Didn't stop yours from opening the trapdoor and breaking his neck."

"My father was just doing his job," Grace said stiffly. She thought back to the conversation she had had with her father about Roger Matthews.

*"I was there when the priest came for Drake's father on the morning he was hanged. He confessed to the theft of the lead and plenty of other things besides."*

"Leave me alone," she told Drake. "I've cakes to buy. And I've no interest in having this conversation."

She turned away from him, hearing a burst of cold laughter in her ear.

"Cakes?" Drake repeated. "You'll be eating stale bread out on the streets this time next year. Won't be long before your father has gambled your house away."

Grace froze. Despite herself, she turned back to look at Drake. "What did you say?"

Drake shrugged "Everyone knows it. Old Llewellyn Dillingham just can't stay away from the gambling halls. They say he's got debts he can hardly pay. They say he's about to lose everything."

She shook her head. "No. That's not true." She heard her voice waver with uncertainty.

"Grace? Are you all right?"

She heard Phillip's voice behind her. Was achingly glad to see him. He stepped close to her, pressing a hand to her shoulder.

"Well now," Drake drawled. "If it ain't Phillip Butler. Trying to be the hero again."

Phillip stepped closer to Drake. "Leave her alone."

Grace chewed her lip. Though Phillip and Drake stood eye to eye, Drake was much wider, his arms much thicker. As much as she hated to admit it, she felt certain he could knock Phillip down with a single blow. Nonetheless, Phillip held Drake's gaze searingly, refusing to be intimidated.

Drake's eyes darted between Phillip and Grace, before seeming to become aware of all the people surrounding them. He turned on his heel and darted out of the market, snatching an apple from a grocer's stall as he passed.

Grace let out her breath in relief. She looked up at Phillip. "What are you doing here?"

"I saw Drake heading for the market as I was leaving. Thought it best I come and find you in case he had a mind to cause trouble."

Grace nodded her thanks. She found herself taking a step closer to Phillip, steadied by his presence. He pressed a hand to her shoulder. "Come on. Buy your cakes and then I'll walk you home."

* * *

AFTER WALKING Grace to the door of her house, Phillip headed home. He dug his hands into his pockets and strode with his head down, drawing deep breaths in an attempt to steady himself. He hated that even after all these years, Drake Matthews still had the ability to rattle him.

But there was something about Drake that set Phillip on edge. A dull awareness that Drake had little regard for right and wrong. And that he would do whatever it took to get the revenge for his father's death he seemed to seek so desperately.

Did Drake truly believe his father was innocent, Phillip wondered. Or was it just something he told himself in order to get through each day? Either way, he wanted nothing more than for Drake to be gone from his life. Wanted even more for him to be gone from Grace's.

When he let himself inside, Phillip found his father sitting at the kitchen table, account books spread out in front of him. Illegible words and figures were scrawled across the pages, punctuated with splatters of ink. Andrew Butler had built his business up from nothing, acting as a property agent to London's middle class and beyond. These days, the houses on his books ranged from tiny Bermondsey cottages to the grand mansions that lined the streets of Mayfair. But the success of the business did not mean his bookkeeping had become any neater.

Andrew was grooming his son to take over the business one day, and when that happened, Phillip felt certain he would have to hire a shorthand expert to decipher his father's scribbles.

Andrew looked up as Phillip approached the table. "What's happened, boy?" he demanded.

Phillip gritted his teeth. He hated that his father could tell with just one look that he was rattled.

When he was a child, Phillip's father had always urged him to stand up for himself more. To be more aggressive, more forceful.

*Be a man*, he had said far too many times. Aggression had never come naturally to Phillip. And more than anything, he hated his father's insinuation that he had to swing his fists in order to be a man. On the day he had come home from school with a black eye courtesy of Drake Matthews, his father had been far too excited.

Still, despite it all, Phillip had always gotten along well with his father. Had always known Andrew only wanted the best for his son. And so, as he sank at the table beside his father, he said, "I had another run-in with Drake Matthews."

"Drake Matthews?" his father repeated, eyes still on his ledger. "What are you doing spending your time around that animal?"

"He was bothering Grace," said Phillip.

"Ah." His father looked at him then and gave him knowing eyes. "I see."

Phillip felt his cheeks colour. He looked down at his father's ledgers, suddenly desperate to steer the conversation in a different direction. "Any new properties on the books, Father?"

But Andrew asked, "Is that really the kind of girl you want as a wife?" He turned his pen around in his fingers. "The hangman's daughter?"

Phillip felt a jolt in his chest. He had never thought of Grace as a potential wife. He had never thought of anyone in that way. Marriage seemed like a faraway prospect, one resigned to the distant future. And yet, as he tossed the thought around in his head, he realised it was a comforting one. Perhaps some unconscious part of him *had* thought of Grace in that way. She had always been there, a part of his life for as long as he could remember. She was his dearest friend and if he allowed himself to acknowledge it, Phillip also realised there was a part of him that longed for her to be more. The realisation was not a surprising one. It merely felt like he was bringing to light something he had always known.

But his father was looking at him expectantly, disapproval in his eyes.

"What does it matter who her father is?" Phillip asked, his words coming out sharper than he had intended.

His father tapped his fingers on the edge of the table in a jagged rhythm that made Phillip grit his teeth in irritation.

"I know the kind of abuse Llewellyn Dillingham suffers each day," said Andrew. "I know what people think of him. You want to associate yourself with all that?"

Phillip said nothing. He knew all too well about that abuse. Had heard endless stories from Grace about paint on their front door, and the insults hurled in the street. He knew these things contributed in no small part to Llewellyn seeking peace at the bottom of a whisky bottle. And, even more dreadfully, they had contributed to Grace's mother taking her own life. But none of that changed how he felt about Grace. He looked squarely at his father.

"I care about Grace very much," he said, his voice growing stronger with each word. "What her father does is no matter to me."

For a moment, Andrew looked taken aback at Phillip's uncharacteristic boldness. He eyed his son for a moment, then turned back to his books and snorted. "You're asking for trouble, boy, I'm telling you. Don't say I didn't warn you."

* * *

THAT NIGHT, as was becoming more and more common, Grace couldn't sleep. She lay in bed, staring into the dark, Drake's words churning through her mind.

*Old Llewellyn Dillingham just can't stay away from the gambling halls.*

*You'll be eating stale bread out on the streets this time next year.*

As much as she longed to convince herself Drake was wrong, she couldn't keep his words from gnawing inside her.

Was there the chance that he was right? Was

her father gambling away the money that he needed to pay for the house? Would they be out on the streets come Christmas?

Deciding sleep was still hours away, Grace climbed out of bed and wrapped her shawl around her shoulders. She would not work herself into a state by lying in the dark and churning over problems that might not even exist. Instead, she would make a start on the bread for supper tomorrow.

As she crept down the passage, she peered into the parlour. Her father was asleep in his favourite armchair, an empty bottle on the floor beside his stockinged feet. Dark circles underlined his eyes, his sand-coloured beard long and unkempt. Grace sighed. At least he wasn't at the tavern tonight, she told herself.

She went to the kitchen and measured out the ingredients for the bread, losing herself in the task of mixing and kneading.

A knock at the door made her start. Who could be paying them a visit at this time of night? Her mind went to the thugs who had thrown the rock through the window some months ago. She would ignore the knocking, she decided. Hoped they would go away. After all, it wouldn't be long before the police came past the house to check on things.

But when the knocking sounded again, Grace heard the creak of her father's armchair. Heard him amble down the hallway and pull open the door.

"I'm in need of good luck, Mr Dillingham," said a gravelly voice that Grace didn't recognise. "They say you can help me with that."

Grace frowned at the man's cryptic words. She wiped her hands on her apron and bent her head around the doorway of the kitchen. The man at the door was dirty and dishevelled, an enormous greatcoat hanging off his shoulders and a haunted look in his eyes. Dark hair hung loose on his shoulders, a dirty beard reaching to the middle of his chest. He looked past Llewellyn, catching sight of her. Her father turned abruptly.

"What on earth are you doing out of bed, Grace?" he snapped. "Go back upstairs."

She tiptoed towards the staircase but stopped on the landing. Her father hadn't looked surprised to see this odd visitor. Perhaps he had even been expecting him. What did the man mean about her father giving him good luck?

She watched her father disappear into the parlour and return with something between his fist. She frowned. Was that rope? Llewellyn held it out to the man at the door.

"This one was used to hang Jesse Spears."

"The highwayman?"

"The very same. It'll bring you more than a little good luck at the card tables. Also cures headaches."

The man at the door hesitated. "How much?"

"Two guineas," said Llewellyn.

The man hesitated. "That's a fair sum."

Llewellyn stared him down. "You'll earn in back it no time at the card tables."

Finally, the man nodded and reached into his pocket. He handed Llewellyn the coins and took the rope before disappearing back into the street.

Grace hurried upstairs before her father could catch sight of her. She climbed back into bed and pulled her blankets to her chin, a sense of dread settling over her. Her father was not a superstitious man. He knew well that a hangman's rope did not bring a person good luck. And it certainly did not cure headaches. He had never been one to prey on other people's desperation. The man at the door was right; two guineas was quite a sum, especially for a length of rope Grace doubted had even come from the scaffold. No doubt it was money the man could ill afford to part with.

What had her father been thinking? Surely he wouldn't do such a thing unless he was desperate himself. Perhaps Drake was right. Perhaps it was only a matter of time before she and her father were huddled on a street corner, eating nothing but stale bread.

## CHAPTER 6

*A*s the years passed, Llewellyn drifted in and out of his own melancholy. Grace had never again seen him selling rope to strangers at the front door, and for that she was grateful. But she couldn't help but wonder whether he had been too ashamed to do it again, or whether he was simply now making his sales outside of the house where he would not be caught by his daughter.

Grace had taken it upon herself to put aside most of her father's wages each week. Over the past four years, the debt collectors had been at their door on more than one occasion. Each time they had managed to scrape together enough pennies to keep their roof over their head, but Grace feared the day would come when they would not be so lucky. She hated what they had been reduced to. And she hated even more that Drake Matthews had been right; her father had been on the verge of losing their house. Grace tried not to think of how close they had come to living on a street corner.

Still, she knew Llewellyn was making an effort to control his drinking. These days, she rarely saw him drunk and they had begun to spend more and more evenings chatting together at the supper table like they used to. In the past year, Llewellyn had travelled regularly to prisons in Essex and Kent for extra work, and he always handed the extra money over to her on his return.

Though Grace knew he was still gambling, she had decided to keep quiet on the issue. She knew her father needed his vices, and as long as there was enough coin to stave off the debt collectors, she would allow him to do what he needed to get through each day. After many long and difficult years, she was beginning to see a hint of the warm and friendly man her father had been, and she couldn't bear to do anything to scare that man away.

.   .   .

THAT AFTERNOON, Grace was walking with Phillip through Hyde Park. Summer was slowly becoming autumn, and the trees overhead blazed with colour.

Phillip had long been a constant in Grace's life, and she was endlessly grateful she had always had him to turn to, particularly in the difficult years after her mother's death, and during the regular visits of the debt collectors. He had always been there, ready to listen when she spoke of missing Veronica, or of the debt collectors' latest visit. Never passing judgement on the days when out of sheer frustration she would speak ill of her father and his gambling.

When Phillip's father – his only living relative – had passed away a year ago, Grace had been only too eager to repay the favour. She had held him in his grief, had stood beside him at the burial. Had helped him empty the wardrobes of his father's clothes and shoes. Phillip and his father had been close, and his death had hit him hard. And now, at just eighteen, he had inherited not only his father's house but his property agency as well.

On the night she had helped him clear the house of his father's things, Phillip had kissed her for the first time. It had been a gentle, chaste kiss that told Grace he was well aware of the impropriety of them sitting together in a lamplit house now empty but for them. Part of her had been concerned he had been acting purely on a flood of emotion, wrought by his father's death. But she had been unable to stop the warmth that had flooded her body at the feel of his lips against her own.

Since that night, they had never again spent the evening alone together. But when they met for their weekly outings – walks in the park or lazy afternoons in the tea houses – their hands were constantly intertwined, their conversation peppered with stolen kisses.

To Grace, this change in their relationship had merely felt like a natural progression. Though they had never spoken of it, a part of her had always known she and Phillip were meant to be together. Kissing him in front of the fire that first night had felt like the most natural act in the world.

"Did you manage to find another housekeeper?" Grace asked as they approached the Serpentine. Ducks swooped down from above and skimmed across the water, sending ripples flying out across the surface of the lake.

Phillip nodded. "I did. A daily with plenty of experience. She's to start next week."

The housekeeper hired by Phillip's father had retired soon after her master's death. Over the past months, Phillip had gone through at least three replacements. The first had run off to get married a few weeks after arriving, the second had decided to leave London, and the third had been so dreadful at her job that Phillip had eaten dry bread for supper rather than force down her charred stew. On several occasions, Grace had taken him home for a meal. At other times she had dropped soup pots and bread loaves at his door, certain Phillip might starve to death if left to his own devices.

Grace smiled. "And this one can cook? More than toast?"

Phillip chuckled. "She can. I had her do a trial for me last night. The stew was utterly edible."

Grace laughed. "Sounds like a definite improvement."

Phillip reached for her hand, squeezing her fingers gently. He stopped walking and looked down to meet her eyes. "Just say the word, Grace, and that house can become yours too."

Grace didn't speak at once. It was not the first

time Phillip had raised the subject of marriage. She adored Phillip, and a part of her wanted nothing more than to be his wife. But she also loved her father. And she was afraid of what it would do to him if she were no longer at home to take care of him. Yes, Llewellyn's drinking had improved greatly in the past few years, but she knew how easy it would be for him to slide back into his old ways without a watchful eye on him.

Llewellyn knew, of course, of Phillip's intentions. One night at the supper table, he had asked for permission to make Grace his wife and Llewellyn had given it without hesitation.

When her father had pressed her on why she had not accepted Phillip's proposal, Grace's answer had been vague and insubstantial. She knew Llewellyn would object if she told him the real reason she was reluctant to marry. Instead, she had garbled out a line about not being certain of her feelings. She hoped Phillip had not caught word of it.

"Grace?" Phillip pushed, reaching down to tuck a strand of blonde hair beneath her bonnet. "What do you say?"

She closed her eyes for a moment. How she hated letting Phillip down like this. "You know how much I care for you," she said. "And being your wife would make me so happy. But…"

"Your father?" His blue eyes were warm and understanding and the sight of them made Grace feel even more guilty.

"I'm sorry, Phillip," she gushed. "I'm just so worried about him. He's not been the same since Mama died, and he's only just managed to get his drinking under control." She stopped walking and looked up at him with wide, apologetic eyes. "I'm sorry. I truly do want to marry you." She ventured a small smile. "Perhaps there's no rush? I'm only seventeen, after all. And perhaps with time, Papa will be able to manage much better on his own."

To her relief, Phillip gave her a warm smile. "Of course," he said. "There's no rush. You know I'll be here waiting. I'll wait for as long as you need."

Impulsively, Grace threw her arms around him and squeezed. "Thank you, Phillip. You truly are such a good man." She pressed a fleeting kiss onto his lips. "Soon," she said. "I promise."

He grinned. "I'll be waiting."

Phillip took her hand again and they began to walk away from the lake. He stopped suddenly. He pressed a hand to Grace's arm and tried to turn her to walk back the way they had come. "Let's go this way."

Grace frowned. "Why? What's—" She stopped abruptly, catching sight of Drake Matthews striding towards them. He was surrounded by five other men, each in the same ragged shirt and boots as Drake. Each with the same dark and soulless look in their eyes.

"Drake," Grace murmured to herself. She looked up at Phillip. "When was the last time you saw him?"

Phillip's eyes were fixed to the men. "It's been some time. More than a year."

Grace's eyes narrowed as Drake approached, hands dug into the pockets of the dirty greatcoat that hung open across his body. She wondered fleetingly if there was a weapon in his pocket.

He gave them a wide grin that did little to lighten his face. Instead, it only served to make him look even more frightening. "Fancy meeting you two here."

"Leave us be, Drake," said Phillip. "We don't want any trouble."

Drake laughed. "Well that's just too bad, ain't it. Because you're going to get trouble anyway."

Grace stiffened, her fingers tightening around Phillip's arm.

Drake jabbed a grimy finger under her nose. "You hear me, Grace Dillingham? You're all going to get what you deserve. You and that murderer of a father of yours." His eyes flashed. "You're all going to burn in hell."

Grace closed her eyes for a moment, forcing herself to breathe. She was not a child anymore. She would not be frightened by Drake Matthews. And she would not for a second entertain these thoughts that her father was a murderer. She had left those behind many years ago.

Phillip slid his arm around her shoulder, pulling her close. They began to walk brusquely down the path, away from Drake and the other men.

"Don't let him bother you," Phillip said, though Grace could hear the thinness of his words. She hated that Drake had always found a way to get under Phillip's skin.

"I'm not bothered," Grace said, forcing a smile. But she could not ignore the bitterness that had come out of his mouth. Though she knew for certain that Drake's father had been guilty of his crimes, Drake had clearly convinced himself of his innocence. And he was still out for retribution. She stepped closer to Phillip, trying to find a little comfort. Drake Matthews and the men he spent his time with, Grace knew well, had the ability to make her life – and her father's – very difficult indeed.

GRACE LET herself into the house and took off her bonnet. The walk in the park had left a warmth in her cheeks, and she had almost managed to forget the uncomfortable encounter with Drake.

She stopped in the doorway of the parlour, surprised to see her father in his armchair. She had not been expecting him home for hours. He sat with both hands wrapped around an unopened whisky bottle, eyes glazed over as he stared into the amber liquid.

Grace put down her bonnet and hurried towards him. "Papa? Are you all right?" She tried to keep her voice light, determined that her father would not catch word of anything that had happened at the park that day.

Llewellyn let out a heavy sigh. "I'm all right, Gracie." He turned the bottle around in his hands.

"No, you're not." Grace sat opposite him in the

other armchair and fixed her eyes on his. "Tell me what's happened?"

Llewellyn hesitated for a moment, as though debating whether or not to speak.

"Papa?" she pressed. "I'm a grown woman now. I ought to know what's going on." She shook her head. "I *need* to know."

That brought a small smile to her father's face. "A grown woman. Indeed you are. And a fine young woman you are too." He placed the whisky bottle on the side table and looked up at Grace. After a long silence, he said, "I'm to hang a woman and her two daughters next week."

Grace couldn't hold back her gasp. "What?"

"They were found guilty of murder," Llewellyn told her bluntly. "They killed the girls' father. They were found at the house covered in his blood and each confessed to the crime. So it's only fair they be sent to the gallows."

Despite her unease, Grace nodded silently. She waited for her father to continue.

"I've always prided myself on being able to keep the prisoners calm," he told her. "An easy death. None of these gruesome theatrics like Calcraft."

Grace nodded again.

"I'm just not sure I have it in me to do the same

for this mother and her daughters," Llewellyn said. "I've never put a woman to death before. Let alone three of them at once. And I couldn't bear it if they were to go to their death struggling or too terrified to stand." He looked up at her, his eyes glowing in the lamplight. "No one deserves that. No matter what they've done."

Grace felt a sudden swell of affection for her father. And a sudden swell of hatred for Drake. Llewellyn Dillingham was an achingly decent man, she thought. How dare Drake say such dreadful things about him?

"I'll do it," she told her father suddenly. "I'll come with you. Make sure the mother and daughters are calm."

Llewellyn shook his head. "No, Grace. Absolutely not. I—"

"Why not?"

"Because I don't want you involved." His voice was firm.

"Please, Papa," she pushed. "You've always said how important it is to keep them calm. I know how much it means to you that the prisoners have an easy death. And I know that this will be difficult for you." She reached for his free hand. "Let me help you. Please. I want to."

For a long time, Llewellyn didn't speak. He tilted the whisky bottle, making the liquid glow orange in the rusty light of the lamp. After a moment, he set the bottle on the table. Gave a slight nod.

"All right. But just this once. This is the life I chose, Grace. These are my struggles. I don't want you to get involved." But even as he spoke, she could hear the relief in his voice.

Grace climbed from her chair and wrapped her arms around him, squeezing him tightly. "Your struggles are my struggles, Papa. We do things together." She lifted the whisky bottle from the table. "May I get rid of this?" she asked, looking him pointedly in the eye.

Her father nodded. "Yes, Gracie. Pour it away."

Grace gave her father a small smile, then carried the bottle out into the yard and emptied the whisky into the garden.

## CHAPTER 7

On Monday morning, Grace accompanied her father to Stepney Prison. Later that week, the mother and daughters were to be put to death and Grace had tasked herself with keeping them calm on the walk to the scaffold. If she was to do that without crumbling, she needed to know exactly what she would be facing. And so today she would witness her father put three other prisoners to death.

"Are you sure about this?" asked Llewellyn as they stepped out of the house into the pearly dawn light. He was dressed in the neat black suit he wore whenever he was to perform a hanging. He held out a hand to hail a cab.

Grace nodded. "I'm sure. I want to help you

with the mother and daughters on Friday, and I want to know what to expect."

Her father gave her a strained smile, but Grace could see the pride in his eyes.

The cab rolled noisily to the edge of the street, wheels hissing against the damp cobbles. Llewellyn offered Grace his hand to help her climb into the coach.

She sat opposite her father, clasping her hands tightly in her lap. Despite herself, Grace was nervous about seeing her father at work. Though she had known for many years exactly what it was he did, she had never before seen him pull the lever of the trapdoor. Had never actually witnessed him send another human being to their death.

*He is just doing his job*, she told herself. But it did not change the fact that he was to take someone's life. Nor did it ease the uncomfortable churning in her stomach.

"Are you all right, Gracie?" Llewellyn asked, a faint frown darkening his face.

She forced a smile. "Of course."

"It's not too late if you want to change your mind."

"No," she said firmly. "I'll not change my mind.

I want to be here. Truly." But she could not quite bring herself to believe it.

THE CAB SLOWED to a halt across the road from the jail and Grace climbed out carefully. She stood for a moment staring up at the building in which her father spent so much of his life.

Stepney Prison was an imposing stone building that rose three storeys and occupied an entire block. Narrow windows dotted the building, looking down on the street like eyes.

Grace followed her father around the side of the building. She caught a glimpse of a burial yard behind the jail; rows of crosses dotting the bare earth.

What a sorry reality, she thought dully, for an executed prisoner to be buried in such a place. To be unable to escape their prison, even in death.

Llewellyn put a hand to her shoulder and led her into the building, nodding to the guard at the door. Inside was cold and dim, the narrow windows doing little to light the interior. Long grey corridors stretched out ahead of them, lined with heavy wooden doors.

Grace's footsteps echoed as she followed her

father down the passage. She realised she was holding her breath.

A feeling of hopelessness pressed down upon the place. A feeling of sadness. Grace found herself thinking of Drake and his hanged father. She glanced up at Llewellyn. What it must be like to work in such a place every day. To be surrounded by such despair, such grief, such fear. Little wonder he had been driven to drink. For a fleeting second, Grace wished her mother had tried harder to convince Llewellyn to step away from his role.

But today, Llewellyn was composed and calm. He led Grace up a narrow stone staircase to the second floor and stopped outside the last door in the passage. The guard waiting outside nodded in greeting.

Llewellyn gestured to Grace. "My daughter will be accompanying me today."

"As you wish, Mr Dillingham," the guard said. He took a large ring of keys from his belt and slid one into the door.

Llewellyn looked back over his shoulder. "Are you certain?" he asked Grace again.

She nodded, though her flimsy resolve had not been helped by the bleak atmosphere of the prison.

On the other side of this door, she knew were the three men due to hang that morning.

The heavy door creaked as it opened. Grace waited for her father to pull on his hood to hide his face from the men he was to kill. But to her surprise, he just stepped into the cell. Grace followed, her heart thudding in her chest.

The three men were huddled together in the far corner of the small cell. Each wore a ragged, colourless shirt, their hair dirty and unkempt. A priest stood beside them, murmuring, clutching the hands of one of the men. Grace heard a muffled sob and realised one of the men was crying. A deep ache tightened her chest and she fought the urge to rush out of the cell.

She watched as her father walked right up to the crying man and pressed a firm hand to his shoulder.

"Have no fear. It will all be over soon. There will be no suffering. And then you will be at peace with the Lord."

The man gave another loud sob, then swallowed his cries. He nodded slowly.

Llewellyn moved quietly between the three prisoners, murmuring his calming words. Grace tried to memorise them.

*Have no fear.*

*It will be over soon.*

*You will be at peace with the Lord.*

She stood with her back pressed to the door, too on edge to venture any closer to the prisoners. But how composed and calm her father seemed. The men were listening as he spoke, nodding, murmuring their responses. Grace hoped that when she faced the mother and daughters at the end of the week, she might do such a good job.

Finally, Llewellyn stepped out of the cell and Grace following.

"It's time," Llewellyn told her. "Do you wish to watch the execution?"

Grace sucked in her breath. A part of her wanted nothing more than to shake her head; to tell her father to simply return for her when the deed was done. But she had come here so she might be prepared. So she might know exactly what to expect when the three women were put to death on Friday. And that meant watching as these men were hanged.

She nodded to her father. "Yes. I want to see it all."

Llewellyn nodded, though Grace could see apprehension in his eyes. Could tell there was a part of him that did not want his daughter to see the things he was about to do. He turned to one of the guards.

"Please take my daughter out to the execution yard."

Grace followed the guard wordlessly, drawing in long deep breaths in an effort to remain calm.

The execution yard at the front of the prison was filled with people, though the crowd was nowhere near as heaving as she had imagined. When Phillip had told her stories of watching William Calcraft's executions at Newgate, he had spoken about crowds of hundreds, if not thousands, shouting and jeering as the prisoners flailed on the ends of the ropes. The thought of it had turned Grace's stomach. How was it that ending a person's life might be such a source of entertainment? Were these people nothing but animals? How could they have so little compassion?

She was glad for the small crowd. And she was certainly glad her father did not have a similar reputation to Calcraft; a string of bungled executions and hangings that were more theatre than the deliverance of justice.

The jail door creaked noisily and Llewellyn stepped out, his face hidden by a large black hood.

A hush fell over the murmuring crowd. And out came the three condemned men, flanked by guards with rifles at the ready. Each of them walked steadily onto the gallows. All three had refused a hood, and though Grace could see fear in their eyes, she could also see something else: a calm acceptance. An acknowledgement that this would all be over soon and then there would be no more suffering.

She felt a sudden swell of pride for her father.

Llewellyn stepped forward, placing a noose around the neck of each man. And then, as calmly and steadily as he had walked onto the scaffold, he pulled each lever. One, two, three.

As the men fell and the rope snagged and pulled tight, Grace felt a jolt in her chest. But her father had been right. Each man had died in seconds. An easy death. No suffering. She looked up at Llewellyn, feeling a tiny smile on the edge of her lips.

FRIDAY CAME TOO QUICKLY. Grace had spent every night that week tossing and turning, hearing the thud of the trapdoor in her dreams. Proud as she had been of her father and his humane method of putting prisoners to death, she feared she would not be strong enough to show the same composure. Not for the first time, she wished she had not agreed to help her father with the mother and daughters. But she could not back out now. She knew Llewellyn was counting on her. And she wanted to please him. Wanted him to be as proud of her as she was of him.

The morning was overcast and grey, giving the wide bulk of the prison an even more dour feel. Perhaps it was fitting, she told herself. Suitable weather for the hanging of three women who had murdered a husband and father.

Grace was silent as she followed her father down the passage of the jail towards the condemned cell. This time, instead of stepping inside, Llewellyn stopped a few yards from the door.

Grace waited for him to ask her if she was certain. Waited for him to try and talk her out of this. But instead, he just offered her a small smile and said, "Thank you, Gracie. You're far stronger than me."

Grace tried to smile in response but found herself unable. She didn't feel strong. She felt like crumpling into a heap and willing herself away from this place. But a part of her was glad for her father's words. They had ensured she could not change her mind now.

She stood motionless for a moment, watching as her father continued towards the door that opened out to the execution yard. Then she drew in her breath and turned to face the guard at the door of the condemned's cell.

"Are you ready, Miss Dillingham?" he asked.

*No*, Grace thought. She was not ready. But she nodded anyway. "Is the priest inside?" she asked.

The guard shook his head. "The women didn't wish to speak with him. They sent him away."

Grace frowned. How could they have sent the priest away on the morning they were to die? Her heart quickened as she realised the job of keeping these women calm upon the scaffold lay squarely on her shoulders.

The guard pulled the door open, allowing her inside.

The three women stood in a circle in the centre of the cell, arms wrapped around each other and heads bowed in murmured conversation. At the sound of Grace's footsteps, they looked up as one to stare at her.

"Who are you?" The question came from the

woman Grace guessed was the mother. She, like her daughters, wore a long, colourless smock, her feet bare and her grey-streaked hair hanging loose around her face. Her eyes were hard and cold. She looked Grace up and down, scrutinising.

Unable to find an answer, Grace's gaze drifted to the two daughters. Each had a long dark plait hanging down their back, their eyes wide and blue. One of the girls Grace guessed to be no older than her. Her sister perhaps a few years older. For a moment, she just stared at the women. They had murdered their father, she reminded herself. Been found covered in his blood and had each confessed to the crime. But as Grace watched them huddle closer together and grip each other's hands, she found it impossible to imagine them doing such a thing. What had driven them to do it, she wondered. Had the man harmed them? Had they been acting to save themselves? Or was she just being naïve? Perhaps these women were cold-blooded killers. Perhaps they, like Drake's father, deserved all that came to them.

"You don't wish to speak with a priest?" she said finally, her voice stuck in her throat.

The mother gave a cold laugh. "A priest. What

good's that going to do us? We're already going to hell."

Grace felt a sudden chill go through her. And in an instant, she was able to imagine it in horrifying detail; that vicious murder, these three women standing over the father's body with blood on their hands. She closed her eyes for a moment, forcing away the urge to scream at the guard to let her out of the cell. Instead, she stepped up to the youngest daughter and reached for her hand. The young woman looked surprised at Grace's gesture but did not pull away. Grace realised the girl's eyes were full of tears.

"It will be a quick death," she said, forcing steadiness into her words. "The hangman will make sure of it. He is very skilled at what he does. There will be no suffering. And then you will be at peace with God."

A part of her expected the mother to bristle at her mention of God but instead, there was silence.

Grace felt the girl's fingers tighten around her own. She looked up at Grace with large blue eyes. Eyes that held regret, guilt, shame, and yes, a great deal of fear.

"No suffering," she said again. This time the girl nodded.

The second daughter took a step closer to Grace. "And it will be over in a second?"

Grace nodded, reaching out and taking her hand too. "Yes. I promise."

The girl managed something close to a smile. "Thank you."

Drawing in her breath, Grace turned back to face the mother. Would this hard-eyed woman accept anything she had to say?

"Over in seconds," the woman said, her words dripping with bitterness. "Won't the crowd be disappointed about that?" she snorted. "Half of London must have come out to see the mad wenches die."

Grace cleared her throat. "There will be a crowd, yes," she said. "But the man who is to perform the execution does not do what he does for the crowd's entertainment. You will not be made a spectacle of."

For a moment, the mother didn't speak. Just stared at Grace with the same piercing blue eyes of her daughters. Grace swallowed hard, feeling tears gather in her throat. These women were murderesses, she reminded herself. They deserved the punishment that was coming to them. But standing there with them, with their fearful eyes boring into her, that fact did not make things any easier. In a few moments, all three would be dead. Those bright blue eyes would grow blank and cold. And her father would be the one to pull the lever.

A sharp rap on the door yanked Grace from her thoughts.

"Time," the guard said sharply.

The youngest daughter gave a muted sob. Grace looked back at her, forcing down her tears. "Be brave," she said. "Remember, you will soon be at peace. All of you."

The door creaked open to reveal two guards, one of them carrying three black hoods in his hand. Grace willed the women to accept them. It would be easier for her father, she knew, if he was unable to see their faces at the moment he pulled the trapdoor's lever. The mother reached out a hand to each of her daughters and the three stepped together from the condemned cell, following the guard out to the execution yard.

"This way, Miss Dillingham," said the second guard. "I'll take you out to the viewing area."

Grace shook her head stiffly. "No." She couldn't do it, she realised. She could not watch these women stand upon the gallows and fall to their death. She could not watch her father end these lives. Guilty or not, the entire practice of putting criminals to death just felt unbearably cruel. These women had killed a man and were to have their lives taken away in return. Didn't that make the courts, the magistrate, the *hangman,* just as guilty? Grace turned abruptly and hurried back through the jail, bursting out onto the street just as her tears spilt down her cheeks.

## CHAPTER 8

*G*race was curled up on her bed when her father returned home that evening. After racing from the jail before the women's execution, she had hailed a cab and cried in the carriage all the way home. She had not prepared supper or cleaned the house. With the fires unlit, the house was dreadfully cold.

But she felt weighed down by sadness. Sadness at the lost lives of the women, and at whatever it was that had made them murder their husband and father. Sadness at all the other prisoners in the condemned cells awaiting their death. And sadness that her loving, decent father might be forced to spend his days among such horror.

She wondered if Llewellyn knew she had not been able to watch the execution. What would he think of her if he knew? She did not blame her father, of course. He had only been doing his job. And she had seen first-hand how good he was at what he did. She hated that he might think that she had been unable to watch out of shame or anger.

She closed her eyes and buried her head in her pillow. She did not want to face her father tonight.

But she could hear his footsteps thudding steadily up the stairs. Could hear him drawing closer to her room. He tapped lightly on the door.

"Gracie? Are you in there?"

Grace sat up. "Yes, Papa." She climbed slowly to her feet, feeling a dull weight pressing down upon her shoulders. She rubbed her eyes and opened the door. "I'm sorry, I've not got supper ready yet. I'm afraid I was—"

But before she could finish speaking, Llewellyn reached out and pulled her into his arms, holding her in a tight embrace. "I'm sorry, Grace," he said. "I should never have let you do that."

She shook her head. "I wanted to." But as she spoke, a fresh flood of tears spilt down her cheeks. Her father pulled her tighter into his arms.

"You didn't watch the execution," he said. "I was worried about you. The guard said you ran out of there as fast as you could manage."

Grace sighed sadly. She pulled out of her father's embrace and sat back on the edge of the bed. "I'm sorry, Papa," she said again. "I just couldn't do it. Not after speaking to those women." She gave him a sorry smile. "I suppose I'm not as strong as you thought I was."

Llewellyn reached his arm around her, kissing the top of her head. "You are one of the strongest people I know."

"I don't know how you do it," Grace admitted. "I don't know how you have the strength to speak to the prisoners and then put them to their deaths so calmly and quickly." She looked up to meet his eyes. "I'm very proud of you."

A faint smile flickered beneath Llewellyn's beard. "I'm very glad to hear you say that, Gracie." His voice dropped slightly. "I was afraid you were ashamed of me. I was afraid that was why you chose not to watch the hanging."

Grace shook her head emphatically. "No. Never." She chewed her lip. "Were the women calm, Papa? Did they go to their deaths quietly?"

Llewellyn nodded. "As calmly as anyone I've seen. And I'm sure that was all thanks to you."

Grace was glad of it. For several moments she said nothing, just twisted the corner of the blanket around her finger. "Do you think it's right, Papa?" she said suddenly.

"Do I think what's right?"

"Putting people to death for their crimes. How do we know what drove those women to kill their husband and father? And what about Roger Matthews? Is a little lead from a church roof really worth a man's life?" She heard her voice rise. "Who are we to decide who lives and who dies?"

She surprised herself with her outburst. How long had these thoughts been hiding in the back of her mind? But yes, the more she thought about them, the more she realised there was merit to them. After all, was it really right that a man could choose whether another person lived or died? Was it really right for anyone to have that kind of power? And how could the world expect men like her father to earn a living in such a way? How was he supposed to live with himself when he went to work each day to send others to their death?

Llewellyn looked at her for a long second, a

tiny smile in the corner of his lips. "That's a dangerous question to ask, Grace," he said. "Though you'd not be the first to do so."

"Dangerous?" she repeated. "Why is it dangerous?"

"Because it's the way things have always been. And when you challenge a practice that has been in place as long as this, there will always be those who passionately oppose you."

"And so we're never to challenge anything?" she asked. "Even if we believe it wrong?" She heard her voice grow stronger. "How is anything ever to change if we don't stand up for what we believe in?"

Llewellyn gave her another smile, but Grace could see the sadness in his eyes. "You sound like your mother."

"Really? Mama believed these things too?"

Llewellyn nodded. "Very much. She hated the way I spent my days. Hated that I was expected to do such a thing. She said that such power should only lie in the hands of God, not a man."

Grace didn't reply. It was the first time in many years she had heard Llewellyn speak of her mother.

"What about you, Papa?" she asked. "Do you agree with Mama? Do you agree with me?"

Llewellyn didn't speak immediately and Grace regretted the question. It wasn't fair, she knew, to ask such things of him. The job he did he had only ever done to support his family.

But before she could speak again, Llewellyn said, "Yes, Grace, I do agree with you. And I wish things were different. I wish I had some other way of earning a living. But I just want the best for you. It's all I've ever wanted."

Grace nodded. "I know, Papa. And I'm grateful." She looked up at him, meeting his eyes. "I'm sorry," she murmured. "I didn't mean to upset you."

"Upset me?" Llewellyn repeated. "Oh Gracie, you've not upset me." He bent to kiss the top of her head. "I think perhaps I've never been more proud of you in my life."

THE FOLLOWING EVENING, Grace set out towards the prison to meet her father after work. Their conversation the previous evening had given her a glimpse at the guilt Llewellyn carried each day as a result of the way he spent his life. And she had experienced first-hand the bleak and crushing atmosphere of the prison. When her father stepped out of the prison gates that day, she wanted to be there waiting for him. Wanted to offer him a warm smile and a little company as he made the journey home.

The sun was beginning to sink as Grace sat in the back of the carriage and peered out the window. The sky was bathed in orange, London's jagged skyline silhouetted against its brightness. But when the coach rounded the corner and the stone monstrosity of Stepney Prison came into view, the colour seemed to drain from the evening.

Grace climbed out of the cab and wrapped her arms around herself, shivering. She wished she had thought to bring a coat.

As she looked up at the building, her stomach rolled. At the sight of the prison, her thoughts were back with the three women who had been sent to their deaths the previous day. She couldn't shake the image of those wide blue eyes staring into hers.

She made her way around the side of the building to the gate where she and her father had entered the previous day.

On the edge of her vision, she could see the

burial yard. Movement there, she realised, stepping closer to the fence to look.

Two gravediggers stood at the edge of the cemetery, shovels in hand and piles of earth beside them. Two bodies lay on a cart beside them, wrapped in colourless sheets. The bodies were small and slight. Grace's breath left her for a moment, as she realised what she was seeing. Female bodies, she felt sure. No doubt they were the women who had been hanged the previous day. But why only two bodies, she wondered. Where was the third?

She squinted in the half-light. Surely she was mistaken. Perhaps the third body had already been buried. She stepped closer, watching the gravediggers as they tossed aside their shovels and made their way to the cart.

She needed to see this, Grace realised. Needed this closure, this assurance that the women's bodies were being duly taken care of, that they were at rest as she had promised them they would be. Perhaps then she could find a little of her own peace. But she could not shake the uncomfortable feeling gnawing beneath her skin.

*Why only two bodies?*

The gravediggers lowered one of the women

into her grave. They tossed earth over the corpse, the dirt sighing softly against the body. Grace squinted, searching for another freshly dug grave in which the third woman might have been buried. She could not find one.

The second body was lowered into the earth and the grave filled in. And then the grave diggers tossed their shovels onto the empty cart and began to drag it back towards the prison.

Grace frowned as she walked back to the gate to wait for Llewellyn. She would ask her father about it this evening, she decided. No doubt he would have a simple explanation for her. Something that would put her mind at ease.

The crunch of hooves and carriage wheels made her look up. A darkly painted wagon was rattling down the street towards the jail, pulled by an enormous black horse. It pulled up alongside a jail gate a little further down the fence from Grace. The coachman climbed from the box seat and spoke to the guard, who nodded and disappeared into the jail.

Moments later, Llewellyn appeared from inside the prison, dressed in his customary black frock coat. He bobbed his head and spoke to the coachman in words Grace couldn't hear. The two men disappeared back into the prison.

When they returned, they were carrying a small figure wrapped in a cloth identical to that covering the two bodies she had just seen buried. Grace stared in disbelief. The third woman, she was suddenly certain. She felt her heartbeat quicken, a feeling of dread beginning to press down on her. What was she witnessing? What was her father doing with the woman's body?

She stared with horror as the body was loaded into the back of the wagon. She watched as the coachmen pulled out a pouch and pressed it into Llewellyn's hands.

Was her father being paid for the body?

With a racing heart, she watched as the coach pulled away from the jail and disappeared into the shadowy street.

On shaky legs, Grace began to walk towards her father. She wanted him to see her. *Needed* him to. And she needed answers.

Llewellyn opened the pouch and shook out a few coins. He counted them silently before tucking them back into his pocket. Then he looked up suddenly, catching sight of his daughter. A look of horror fell across his face. A look of inescapable guilt.

"Grace," he began. "I—"

But she did not stay to hear his explanation. Suddenly, she did not want answers. Suddenly, all she wanted was to be as far away from her father as possible.

## CHAPTER 9

*G*race tore away from the prison and onto the high street. She waved her arm frantically in an attempt to hail a cab. When a carriage pulled to the side of the road, she scrambled in frantically, desperate to leave Stepney before her father caught up with her.

By the time she reached home, her lungs were blazing and tears burned her eyes. She raced towards the staircase and thundered up to her bedroom. Her father could make his own supper tonight, she told herself. How could she sit across the table from him after she had watched him sell the woman's body?

To her horror, it was only minutes before she heard the front door slam. Llewellyn's footsteps hurried up the stairs. He knocked frantically on her bedroom door and let himself in before she could respond.

"Grace," he tried again. "I'm so sorry. I never meant for—"

"Who was that?" she demanded, unwilling to hear her father's miserable explanation. "Was that the girl who…" She couldn't find the words. "The girl from yesterday…"

Her father nodded guiltily. "Yes, Grace. I'm sorry. I—"

"What were you doing with her body?" Grace cried. "Who was the man in the coach?" She could feel herself growing hot with anger. What a fool she had been, assuming her father felt guilty for the things he did. And all the while he was selling the bodies of the people he executed. How many years had she spent convincing the world of her father's decency? She felt completely betrayed.

How long had this been going on? How much more was there to know about her father? What other dreadful things had been happening behind her back?

Llewellyn rubbed his eyes. His shoulders were hunched, his eyes on the floor. Grace had never seen him look so ashamed. Was it shame over what he had done? Or regret that he had been caught in the act? Grace glared up at him with hot eyes, wordlessly demanding an explanation.

"The man in the coach was the assistant to an anatomist," Llewellyn told her finally.

"An anatomist?" Grace repeated.

"Yes. He studies the human body, and—"

"I know what an anatomist is," she snapped. She folded her arms across her chest.

"Anatomists use the corpses for research," Llewellyn told her. "They can learn a great deal by studying the bodies of those that have recently died."

Grace felt tears welling behind her eyes. All she could think about was the youngest of the two daughters. Was it her body Llewellyn had sold to the anatomist? She couldn't shake the image of her lying on an examination table, stripped of every inch of her dignity.

"No doubt the anatomist pays well for a young woman," she said bitterly.

Llewellyn didn't answer. Nor did she need him to.

"This is illegal," said Grace. "Isn't it." It was not a question.

Her father sighed and shook his head. Then he

raised his eyes. "Yes," he said heavily. "The law allows some provision, for matters of science. But I should not get personal reward and there is due process to follow. It's very complicated and it's often easier for the anatomist to bypass the paperwork."

Grace's tears spilt suddenly. Who was she crying for? The young woman whose body would be cut to pieces in the name of science? Or was she crying for her father, who had stooped lower than she had ever believed him capable?

"Why would you do this?" she asked finally, swiping angrily at her tears with the back of her hand. "Why would you break the law? If you get caught you'll be severely punished." Her voice began to rise. "You'd likely face the hangman yourself."

Llewellyn nodded wordlessly. "I'm so sorry, Grace," he said, his voice low. "I needed the money. I've debts that need to be paid. And the anatomist, he said he'd pay a handsome sum for..." His voice trailed off as he spoke. "I couldn't bear to lose the house. If I was unable to give you the life you deserved..." He tried to meet her eyes but looked away quickly when he saw the anger in them. "I couldn't bear to see you suffer because of my failures."

For a long time, Grace didn't speak. Her thoughts knocked around inside her head; a tangle of grief and anger and bitter disappointment.

"I've been putting money aside," she said. "I thought it was enough."

Llewellyn's eyes were on the ground. "There are debts," he said after a moment.

"Gambling debts?"

"Yes."

She gritted her teeth. "Was this the first time?" she dared to ask finally.

"No," Llewellyn said, his voice little more than a whisper.

Grace clenched her teeth, unable to look at him. "I would rather you had lost the house," she told him. "I would rather you lost everything we have at the gambling tables than find out you were doing this." She looked up at him, clenching her hands into angry fists. "What about all the things you said yesterday? You told me you agreed with the things I said. You mean to say we don't have the right to decide who lives and dies? But we have the right to do whatever we wish with their bodies once they're gone?" Her eyes hardened. "I promised those women they would find peace in their death. How can that ever be the case when they're to do be carved up on the anatomist's table?"

Llewellyn shook his head. "That young woman is at peace now. I'm sure of it. What happens to her body is of little consequence."

Grace shook her head vehemently. "You don't know that. How can any of us know that?"

Suddenly unable to stay in the house any longer, she rushed from the room, grabbed her coat from the hook and disappeared out into the street.

THE WIND BEGAN to pick up as she strode towards the river. Despite the late hour, the streets were busy and she wove her way through the people clustered on the bridge who were laughing and chattering and peering down at the dark river below. She hurried past Saint Martin's, not slowing until she reached Phillip's neat corner townhouse a few hundred yards from the church.

She rapped on the door, bouncing impatiently on her toes. Not a single part of her cared how inappropriate it was for her to be turning up alone at her beloved's door like this. All she cared about was seeing him. Right now.

His footsteps sounded down the passage and he opened the door, eyebrows rising in surprise at the sight of her.

"Grace," he began. "What are you doing here?"

She threw herself into his embrace, squeezing tightly and felt a little of the anger inside her begin to fade at the feel of his arms around her.

"Let's get married," she told him. "Right away. I'm ready."

Phillip eased her away from him holding her at arm's length. "What's happened, Gracie?" A faint frown creased the bridge of his nose.

She forced a smile, though she could tell her eyes were still red and swollen with tears. "Nothing's happened. I'm ready to be your wife. We've already waited far too long."

Phillip opened his mouth to speak and then decided against it. He took her arm and led her into the parlour, easing her gently onto the sofa. He tucked a strand of hair behind her ear, and only then did Grace realise she had gone tearing out of the house without her bonnet.

He bent to kiss the top of her head. "I'll make us some tea," he told her gently. "Stay here. The housekeeper is off for the night." He tossed another log on the crackling fire and then headed for the kitchen.

He returned moments later with a teapot and two cups which he set on the side table and then sat beside Grace on the sofa. He filled the cups carefully and handed one to her.

Grace wrapped her hands around the cup, savouring its warmth. She took a small sip, the tea going some way to steadying her chaotic thoughts.

Phillip swallowed a mouthful of his own. "Tell me what's happened," he coaxed after a moment.

Grace sighed. "My father," she began. "I caught him doing something dreadful."

She recounted the story to Phillip, feeling the sting of her words. Her father's betrayal stung.

"Selling bodies?" Phillip repeated, surprise in his tone. "Why? Did he need the money?"

Grace nodded sadly. "He says he has debts to pay." She stared into her tea. "Debts that came from the gambling halls." She sighed heavily. "I thought he was doing better. I thought our money troubles were over. I thought I was putting enough away each month. And now I find out he's been selling bodies to the anatomist..."

Phillip reached out and took her free hand. "I'm

sorry, Grace." He peered at her tentatively. "You know he was only doing what he did for you. So you could have the decent life he wants for you."

"I know that," she said. "But it doesn't change what he did. That doesn't change the fact that that poor woman's body is now lying on some table in the Barber Surgeon's Hall, about to be carved up for all to see."

"That poor woman was a murderer," Phillip reminded her.

Grace forced down a mouthful of tea. He was right, of course. But it didn't change the way she felt about the issue.

"I'd rather be living on the streets than know my father was earning money in such a dreadful way."

Phillip smiled gently. "Perhaps you'd not be saying such things if you were huddled in an alley without a roof over your head."

Grace said nothing and, although a part of her was grateful for Phillip's level-headedness, a part of her was angry with him. She didn't want him to take Llewellyn's side. She wanted him to be just as angry. To feel just as betrayed.

"I don't want anything to do with my father anymore," she told him bitterly. "If it weren't for him, you and I would have been married months ago." She shuffled along the sofa until her knee pressed against his. "I don't want to waste any more time."

Phillip smiled, bringing her hand to his lips and kissing her fingers gently. "Grace," he began, "you know I'd marry you in an instant. Nothing would make me happier. But I'll not do it now."

She frowned. "Why not?"

"Because you're angry," he said. "You're emotional. And you're not thinking clearly. I know you're upset with your father. And I would be too. But we have our whole lives ahead of us. I'm not going to rush into marrying you while you're feeling this way."

Grace felt fresh tears welling behind her eyes. As much as Phillip's words disappointed her, she knew he was right.

"I know your father let you down," he said, running a gentle finger over her knuckles. "But he needs you. Perhaps now more than ever."

Grace rubbed her eyes. Llewellyn did need her, she told herself. He was falling apart. Who knew what state he would end up in if he was left to his own devices? Despite her anger at him, Grace knew she could not walk away. She would not leave him on his own to carry his guilt. She knew there was every chance that when she finally returned to the house tonight, she would find Llewellyn at the bottom of a rum bottle. The drink had always been his way to cope with difficult situations.

She sighed heavily. "I ought to go back home. I ought to make sure he's all right."

Phillip smiled, leaning forward and planting a gentle kiss on her lips. "I'll walk you. Let me fetch my coat."

## CHAPTER 10

*T*ry as she did, Grace could not move past her father's betrayal. She could not look at him without seeing him huddled outside the prison taking money from the anatomist's assistant. Could not shake the image of the young woman's body being hauled into the back of that black wagon.

In the week after she had caught him in the act, they had barely spoken a word to each other; Grace was too angry to speak, and Llewellyn, she guessed was either too ashamed or unwilling to battle through her iciness.

The coldness stretched into weeks and then months. Where once they had chatted endlessly at the supper table or by the fire in the parlour, there was now only silence.

Grace couldn't help but be taken back to those dreadful months and years after her mother had died.

She had not been surprised when Llewellyn had returned to the drink. As she had told Phillip on the night she had run to his house, it had always been her father's way of coping.

Some nights she was glad when her father stayed out until all hours at the taverns. It eased the cold and stilted atmosphere that hung over them at the house.

On other nights it just made her sad and lonely.

Although a part of her wanted nothing more than to resurrect their relationship, she found herself unable. On the day she had caught him selling the woman's body to the anatomist, Grace had come to realise that the father she loved so dearly was not the man she had believed him to be.

Phillip, however, was everything she had ever dreamed of in a husband-to-be. He would calmly sit through her angry rants about her father, and offer advice that always managed to soothe her. He would always manage to cheer her up when she was feeling despondent. And though it had been more than a year since he had first spoken of marriage, he was endlessly patient about the matter. Had promised her on more than one occasion that he would give her all the time she needed.

"I will wait for you forever if I have to," he'd told her, holding his lips to hers. And Grace had smiled against his kiss.

"I promise you it won't be that long."

That morning, she stepped out of the house to find him waiting patiently outside. He had planned an outing to the Pleasure Gardens, and Grace was achingly grateful for it. A day boating on the lake was exactly what she needed to take her mind off the coldness of her day-to-day life with her father.

Grace stepped out of the house and pulled the door closed. Llewellyn had left for the prison early that morning and she had not even said goodbye. But at the sight of Phillip waiting in the street, hands dug into the pockets of his coat and his sand-coloured hair blowing across one eye, Grace felt herself break into a smile. Felt a little of the tension vanish from her body.

He offered her his arm and they walked towards the high street for a cab. "Are you all right?" he asked.

She shrugged slightly. "I'm better now that I'm with you."

"Things still difficult with your father?"

Grace said nothing. She knew she didn't need to. Phillip knew her so well that he could read every nuance of her face. But she did not want to speak about her father today. Did not want to think of him. She just wanted to enjoy herself with the man she loved.

"Let's speak of something else," she told Phillip. "Tell me about the business. Have you the royal palaces on your books yet?"

Phillip chuckled. "Not quite. But I've just signed on a client in Belgravia. His parlour is the size of my house."

Grace grinned. "I'm so proud of you. It will be the royal palaces before you know it."

Phillip laughed. "Perhaps one day." A coach rattled towards them and he waved to hail it. He offered Grace a hand to help her to climb inside.

When they climbed from the coach at the Pleasure Gardens, the sun was high and bright. Just a few clouds interrupted the searing blue of the summer sky. Grace lifted her face upwards, enjoying the warmth on her cheeks.

Phillip slid his hand into hers and they walked

through the gardens, admiring the bright rows of roses growing neatly around the edge of a small pond. Hedges rimmed the garden, barely a leaf out of place. Ahead, the surface of the lake shimmered in the sunlight.

Phillip led her to the edge of the water and she smiled at the sight of the small wooden rowboats dotting the surface.

She looked up at him with a smile. "Are you sure you know how to row?"

Phillip winked at her. "I'm sure I'll work it out."

Grace laughed, shaking her head. "There'll be all manner of trouble if we end up having to wade back to shore."

Phillip tugged her towards the jetty, grinning. "If that happens, I promise I'll carry you out on my shoulders." He handed the man on the jetty a few coins and held out a hand to help Grace climb into the boat. She perched tentatively on the bench seat, feeling the boat sway beneath her. Phillip slid onto the seat opposite her and took up the oars. The man on the jetty unwound the rope securing them and pushed them away from their moorings. Soon they were gliding out into the centre of the lake, the oars sighing rhythmically through the water.

Grace smiled as Phillip rowed them further and further from the jetty. He had slung his jacket over the bench seat and his shirt sleeves were rolled up to his elbows. She watched the muscles in his arms tense each time he pulled on the oars. "Look at you. You're a born sailor."

He grinned. "I told you I'd work it out."

She laughed and closed her eyes, leaning back against the edge of the boat to feel the warmth of the sun against her face. With her eyes closed, the sounds around her seemed to grow louder; the twittering of birds in the trees surrounding the lake, the gentle sigh of the oars, a joyful laugh rising up from one of the other rowers. Her every muscle felt soft and relaxed, and her head was pleasantly empty for the first time in as long as she could remember.

When she opened her eyes, Phillip was watching her. Grace could see the adoration in his eyes and it made something warm in her chest.

"What is it?" she asked, her cheeks colouring slightly at the intensity of his gaze.

He shrugged. "I've just not seen you this relaxed in months. It's good to see."

Grace smiled. "I've not felt this relaxed in months." Nor had she stopped thinking about her father for this long before. It was a blissful, liberating feeling. Perhaps it was time, she realised. Time to step away from Llewellyn and live her own life.

After all, what good was it doing either of them for her to be living at the house? She and Llewellyn barely spoke these days, and the atmosphere in the house was almost as cold and uninviting as it was at Stepney Prison. Her presence had not been enough to stop Llewellyn from turning back to the bottle. In fact, it had likely made things worse. These days, Grace was unable to look at her father without thinking of the way he had sold the young woman's body to the anatomist – and she knew that disappointment showed in her eyes. Knew her father was well aware of the way she felt. No doubt it would be better for both of them to have a little space. Space for Grace to try and overcome her disappointment at her father. And space for Llewellyn to live his life without seeing the judging eyes of his daughter each time he sat at the supper table.

Grace sat up suddenly.

"I'm ready," she told Phillip.

He raised his eyebrows. "Ready for what?"

Grace shuffled forward on the bench seat. She

reached for the oar, covering Phillip's hand with hers. "I'm ready to be your wife. I'm ready to start our life together."

Phillip's face broke into a broad smile, his blue eyes shining. "Are you certain?"

"Yes. I'm certain. There's nothing I want more."

"What about your father?"

"It's better this way," Grace told him. "Better for us to have a little space from one another. Perhaps this is something I should have done months ago."

Phillip pulled up the oars, letting the boat drift pleasantly on the lake. He slid forward so his knees were pressed against Grace's. He clasped her hands in both of his. Pulled her close and held his lips gently against hers. "We're going to be so happy, Gracie. We're going to have the most wonderful life together."

THE NEXT MORNING, Grace came downstairs to find her father sprawled in his armchair. He was snoring heavily, still dressed in the stained waistcoat and trousers he had worn the previous day. He had not even removed his boots. Grace stood in the doorway, watching him with an ache in her chest. His beard was long and unkempt, and she could smell the stale odour of liquor and sweat on him.

For a moment, she hesitated. Could she really marry Phillip and leave her father on his own? Was this man truly capable of caring for himself?

She shook the thought away. She'd had this argument with herself many times. And yesterday the decision had been made. She and Llewellyn would be better off with a little distance between them.

When she'd returned home from the Pleasure Gardens the previous evening still buzzing with joy, she had stepped inside to find an empty house. A part of her had been relieved. Though she knew Llewellyn thought well of Phillip and wanted her to be happy, she was not certain how he would react when he learned he was soon to fend for himself. It was a conversation she was not quite ready to have. She had been almost glad when she had the place to herself all evening. She had not even heard her father return from the tavern.

*Today*, she'd thought when she'd woken that morning. Today she would tell her father her news. But now, standing in the doorway of the parlour, staring down at Llewellyn's snoring form, her only thoughts were that she needed to haul him out of this stupor and send him off to work.

She knelt by his side, shaking his arm; gently at first, then harder.

"Papa," she hissed.

Llewellyn opened his eyes with a snort, rubbing a gnarled red hand over his face. "Gracie? What time is it?"

"It's morning," she said. "You're going to be late for work."

"Ah. Work." Llewellyn got unsteadily to his feet. "All right," he said. "I'll get my coat."

Grace gripped her father's arms. "Go upstairs and clean yourself," she said firmly. "Change your clothes. And I'll make you some tea and breakfast."

Llewellyn nodded like a scolded schoolboy and trudged upstairs to his bedroom. Grace watched with a sigh and then headed to the kitchen to heat the kettle.

When her father came back downstairs, his eyes were bloodshot and underlined with shadow but his skin had been scrubbed clean and he was wearing a neat white shirt and his black suit. Grace glanced sideways at the buttons down his chest. She remembered looking at those buttons as a girl, admiring how they shone. These days, they looked tarnished and dull.

But she gave him a small smile, sliding a steaming cup of tea across the table towards him. "That's better," she said. "Much better."

Llewellyn sighed, rubbing his eyes. "I'm sorry, Gracie. I—"

She shook her head, silencing him. This was a conversation they had had so many times she could not find the energy for it anymore. Instead, she sat beside her father and said, "There's a hanging today?"

He nodded. "A young man. Caught thieving from a cobbler." He sighed. "He told the courts he was only stealing so he could keep his house. Keep a roof over his family's head. And now he's to die for it. What's to happen to his family now?"

Grace's heart lurched. The weight pressing down on her father seemed almost physical. How well was he doing these days, she wondered, when it came to keeping these prisoners calm on the scaffold.

"Let me come with you," she said suddenly. "Let me speak to the prisoner before he's hanged."

Llewellyn shook his head. "No," he said. "I don't

want you coming with me to the prison anymore. Not after..." He trailed off.

"Why?" Grace looked at him pointedly. "Are you hiding things?" Instantly, she regretted her words. She saw the sting of them in her father's eyes.

But he said, "No, I'm not hiding anything. I just remember how much it affected you when you spoke to the young women before their executions."

"But they went calmly to their deaths," she reminded him. "I did a good job."

Llewellyn nodded acceptingly. "You did. Yes."

Impulsively, she reached out and grabbed her father's hand. It had been a long time since she had done such a thing and she was surprised by how leathery and rough his skin felt beneath her own. "Keeping this man calm will be difficult for you," said Grace. "I can tell. You don't believe he ought to be executed." She held his gaze. "And you're not at your sharpest this morning. You've had far too much liquor and far too little sleep."

Llewellyn said nothing. But Grace didn't need the confirmation.

"I'm coming with you," she said again.

This time, Llewelyn didn't argue. He just

nodded, tossed back his tea and went out to the hallway for his coat.

AS THEY CLIMBED from the cab outside Stepney Prison, Grace felt nerves begin to bubble up inside her. At the sight of the imposing grey building, she was standing outside the gates again watching her father and the coachman load the young woman's body into the anatomist's carriage.

She closed her eyes for a moment, forcing the memory away. She didn't want to be caught in the past any longer. She wanted only to focus on the future; the life she would create with Phillip and the family they would have. And the relationship she would rebuild with her father.

But as they walked towards the side entrance, Llewellyn said, "I promise the body will be buried. As it should be."

And Grace had no doubt his thoughts had been in the same place as hers had been.

"I know, Papa," she said. "I know."

Despite the drinking and gambling, Grace trusted her father. Knew he had not sold another body to the anatomist since the day she had caught him. His guilt over the incident had been far too striking. But she wished he hadn't felt the need to raise the issue. All she wanted was to forget.

It had been more than a year since Grace had walked the gloomy stone corridors of the prison, but the moment she stepped inside it felt as though no time at all had passed. The jail felt exactly as it had the first time she had entered; the air thick with grief and fear and regret.

Llewellyn led her up the winding staircase towards the condemned cell and Grace's stomach fluttered, hit with a pang of nerves. She pressed her shoulders back and lifted her chin, determined not to let her father see her uncertainty. When they reached the condemned cell, Grace turned resolutely to her father.

"I can do this," she said. She turned to look at the guard. "Let me inside." She stepped into the cell without looking back at Llewellyn.

The man inside was pacing back and forth, murmuring what Grace guessed was a prayer. At the sight of her, he stopped pacing.

He was just a few years older than her, Grace guessed, with large, dark eyes and a face that would have been handsome if it were not so twisted with anguish and fear. At the sight of him, she felt that old anxiousness rear up inside her.

Who were they to choose who lived or died? Who were they to wield such power? This man had stolen only to keep a roof over his family's head. Did he truly deserve to die for such a thing? Did his family deserve to lose their husband and father, merely because they lived in poverty?

Grace wrestled the thought from her head. There was no place for it here now. It would only make this far more difficult. Rightly or wrongly, the courts had made their decision. This man was to die. And he was to do so at the hands of her father.

She took a few slow steps towards the prisoner. "I'm sorry for all that has happened to you," she said. "But I'm here to assure you that your death will be quick. The hangman will make sure you do not suffer at all."

GRACE WAITED outside the execution yard for her father. The young prisoner had gone to his death calmly and quietly and the hanging had been over in seconds. But it did not stop the feeling of hollowness that had opened up inside her. What would become of the young man's family now, she wondered. Would they be forced to live on the streets? Did he have children who would turn to crime too in order to survive? Would they follow their father to the gallows in a few years?

She rubbed her eyes firmly as though by doing so she might scrub those uncomfortable thoughts from her mind. Did her father think similar thoughts, she wondered. Did he consider the families of every criminal he hanged? Or had he learnt to disconnect himself from such things? Grace hoped it was the latter. She could hardly imagine what it would be like to carry such a weight around each day.

She turned her thoughts to Phillip and their upcoming wedding. It brought a smile to her face and instantly lifted the dark cloud that had begun to press down upon her.

"What are you smiling at, Gracie?"

She started at the sound of her father's voice. She had not even heard him approach. For a moment she felt guilty that he had caught her looking so pleased. It felt wrong to be doing such a thing here, standing outside the gates of the execution yard. But her father had a smile of his own. Grace could tell it pleased him to see her happy. At once, the nerves she felt about telling him about her marriage vanished.

"I've something to tell you, Papa," she said suddenly. "Phillip and I are to be married."

Llewellyn's face lit up suddenly and he pulled her into his arms. Grace was taken aback. Her father had not held her in that way in more than a year. It made her realise how much she had missed him.

"Oh Grace," he said, "I'm so pleased to hear that." He stepped back, taking her hand in his and squeezing gently. His face was bright and he looked happier than he had in months. Perhaps years. "Phillip is a fine young man," he said. "I know the two of you will be very happy together."

Grace ventured a smile. "We will, I'm sure."

"When are you to marry?" asked Llewellyn.

"Perhaps a month," Grace told him. "We decided yesterday that that ought to give us enough time to prepare." She tightened her grip on her father's hand. "What about you, Papa? Will you be all right on your own?"

Llewellyn flapped his free hand dismissively. "Oh Gracie, there's no need to worry about me. I can look after myself. I'm a grown man after all." He winked at her. "You'll just have to come and make me your mother's pound cake from time to time."

"Whenever you want it," Grace promised. She felt a warmth inside her. She had not felt this connected to her father in months. She looked up, meeting his gaze. "You're certain?"

"Gracie," said Llewellyn, "all I've ever wanted was for you to be happy and to have a good life. I know I've not always gone about that in the best way, but nothing in the world would make me happier than to see you and Phillip with a family of your own."

Grace swallowed heavily, a lump in her throat. "Thank you, Papa." She squeezed his hand once again, then nodded back towards the jail. "You ought to go back to work. I can make my own way home." She flashed him a smile. "Perhaps I'll make some of Mama's pound cake tonight."

## CHAPTER 11

For the first time in months, Grace was happy. Every morning she woke filled with a sense of excitement at the prospect of becoming Phillip's wife.

As the wedding approached, she spent her evenings ensuring her father knew all he needed to know about fending for himself; how to control the heat of the range, how to make the perfect cup of tea, the ingredients of his favourite beef stew.

"I'll come and make it for you every week," she told him. "But this is just in case you want to try on your own."

Llewellyn had given her a handsome sum to have a dress made for the wedding. At first, she had protested.

"No, Papa. I can't spend all this. I've plenty of dresses I can wear."

But Llewellyn had been adamant. "Let a man buy his daughter a wedding gown, Gracie. Heaven knows you deserve it."

Now, as Grace stood in front of the mirror in the seamstress's parlour, she was glad she had allowed her father to change her mind.

She had chosen pale blue silk for the gown, with delicate embroidery at the neckline. It fastened with a neat row of hooks at her back and had fine pleating at her waist. She had never worn anything so fine. The dress made her feel like a princess. She couldn't wait for Phillip to see her in it.

The seamstress stepped back as she finished her final adjustments.

"There," she said. "Perfect."

Grace smiled at her reflection. "It is perfect. Thank you so much." She felt a fresh rush of excitement along with a tiny flicker of nerves. In a week she was to become a wife. And perhaps soon after that, a mother. Soon she would have her own family to take care of. The thought was thrilling, if a little overwhelming.

The seamstress helped Grace out of her dress and packed it neatly into a large box. She gave Grace a broad smile as she handed it over. "I hope you and your husband-to-be have a very happy life together."

Thanking her again, Grace left the seamstress's and stepped out into the street. The light was beginning to drain from the day, long grey shadows lying over the city. There was a chill in the wind that had not been there when she had stepped inside the dressmakers.

The dress box held to her chest, Grace strode down the street in search of a cab. She couldn't wait to get home and show her father the dress.

She stopped walking suddenly. There, on the other side of the road, was Drake Matthews. Grace felt a stab of fear go through her.

He was following her. He had to be. This city was far too big for these meetings to be coincidental.

A part of her longed to confront him. Ask him what he hoped to achieve by trailing her. By trailing Phillip. After all, it would not bring his father back. It would not change the past. Drake seemed utterly consumed with anger and bitterness. His dark coat was dirty, his boots unpolished. His hair was overgrown and his thick stubble unshorn. She could tell he took not an ounce of pride in his appearance. The sight of him left Grace in no doubt that he was still deeply entrenched in crime. It almost felt as though he was determined to follow in his father's footsteps.

But despite her curiosity, Grace did not want to speak to him. Especially not when she was alone, with the sun beginning to slip below the horizon. She put her head down and began to walk, the box containing her dress held tight against her chest. She prayed a cab would pass soon for her to hail.

She could hear footsteps behind her and knew they belonged to Drake. Could feel his presence pressing down on her. Could feel him getting closer.

"Why are you running from me, Grace?" he asked finally, punctuating the question with a cold and humourless laugh.

"Leave me alone, Drake," she said without looking at him. She kept striding down the foot-path, aware she was heading in the wrong direction. But she did not want to turn off the main street into the narrow alleys that wound down towards the river. Did not want to be alone with Drake Matthews. Perhaps he wasn't even alone, she thought suddenly. Perhaps he was with those dreadful men she had seen him with at Hyde Park. Perhaps they were hiding just out of view, ready to grab her and—

She shook her head violently to stop the thought from progressing.

Drake's footsteps grew suddenly louder, suddenly faster. Suddenly, Grace felt him yanking on her arm. She whirled around involuntarily, the box in her arms spilling onto the footpath. The lid flew off and the delicate silk folds of the gown fluttered into the muck of the street.

Furious, Grace dropped to her knees. She gathered up the dress and shoved the lid back on the box.

"That's a fine gown you got there," Drake sneered, bending over to watch her closely.

Grace got hurriedly to her feet. Drake towered over her.

"A fine gown," he repeated, rubbing the dark stubble on his chin. "But then you always were taken care of, weren't you?" He nodded to the box. "Was that paid for by Papa? Did he buy you a new gown with all that blood money earned by taking innocent lives?"

Grace clenched her teeth, forcing her anger down. How dare he say such things about her father? And how dare he taint her bridal gown with such thoughts? The dress she had chosen to begin this new chapter of her life in.

"Leave me alone, Drake," she said, forcing steadiness into her voice. "I'm not going to have this conversation with you. Not again."

She began to walk, exhaling in relief at the sight of an empty cab clattering up the road. She waved frantically and hurried towards it, scrambling into the coach without looking back at Drake.

GRACE WAS NOT surprised to see the red paint on the door the next morning. She had heard the footsteps outside the house late at night. And now as she stood outside the house in the brisk morning air, staring at the violent red stripe dashed across the door, there was no doubt in her mind as to who the culprit was.

She folded her arms, eyes fixed to the paint. The first time she had seen it, back when she was a child, the sight of the red stripe on the door had terrified her. Now it just made her angry.

Once, she had felt more than a small flicker of pity for Drake Matthews. She had even felt guilty that it had been her own father who had sent him to his death. But that pity and that guilt had long since disappeared.

Something had to be done about Drake. Something had to change. She could not go through the rest of her life dodging him and his gang in the street. Nor could Phillip.

And her father could not spend the rest of his life scrubbing red paint from his door.

Drake had to be stopped.

The thought had begun to bubble inside her during the night while she had sat on her bed and angrily sponged the mud from the skirts of her wedding gown. And now, as she went to the kitchen cupboard for the paint and brush, it was growing in intensity.

*Drake has to be stopped.*

But what was to be done? Short of catching Drake during the committing of the crime, she could hardly go to the police. What would they care that he had knocked her new gown from her hands? Or that he had a knack for appearing just when she didn't want him to? They would put it down to little more than coincidence. But she had to do something. Try as she had to act unafraid, Grace couldn't deny that the sight of Drake Matthews terrified her. She had no idea what he was capable of.

Rifling through the kitchen cupboard, she pulled out the green paint her father had used to paint the front door. If she acted quickly, she could have the red paint covered over before her father woke.

But when she stepped out of the kitchen with the paintbrush in her hand, she found Llewellyn at the bottom of the staircase. His eyes fell to the paint tin in her hand.

"Again?" he asked.

Grace nodded.

Llewellyn sighed. "Leave it, Gracie. I'll fix it before I go."

"It's all right," she told him. "I don't mind." And out she went to the front of the house before her father could speak again. She prised the lid from the paint tin and began to cover the red stripe. With each stroke of the brush, she could feel her anger growing. She would put an end to the torment by Drake Matthews one way or another.

"I DON'T KNOW, GRACE," said Phillip that night. "Send the police after him? Surely that will just cause more trouble. And what proof do we have about any of this?"

Grace was pacing back and forth across Phillip's parlour, her shoes clicking loudly on the floorboards. She couldn't pretend to be surprised by Phillip's reaction, of course. She had the same doubts about being taken seriously by the police. But she had churned the issue over in her mind throughout the day. And going to the police felt like their only option. With her mind made up, she had headed for Phillip's townhouse the moment she knew he had finished work.

"And so what?" she demanded. "We're just to let him follow us for the rest of our lives? Is that what you want for us?" She heard her voice rise. "Is that what you want for our children?"

Phillip held her shoulders to stop her from pacing. "Of course that's not what I want. But what good will going to the police do? You've no proof he was the one to put the paint on your door."

"He was *following* me, Phillip," she told him again. "I know he was. He's been following us for years, just wanting to make our lives miserable."

Phillip nodded slightly. "I know. But we're not going to let him."

Grace met his eyes. "He scared me yesterday. I was afraid of what he might do. I know he blames my family for his father's death."

Phillip let out a long breath. He sank into the sofa and stared into the unlit grate. He rubbed his freshly shorn chin, deep in thought.

"Do the police still patrol outside your house?" he asked finally.

Grace nodded. "But Drake must have waited until they'd gone to paint the door last night."

"Perhaps we give the patrolling officers Drake's name," said Phillip. "Let them know our suspicions." He reached for Grace's hand, tugging her down beside him. "Without proof, I'm afraid there's little more we can do."

Grace sighed. It felt as though Drake deserved far more of a punishment. But she knew Phillip was right. She leaned her head against his shoulder, allowing the feel of his body beneath her to still a little of the anxiety churning in her stomach.

"Does your father know you're here?" asked Phillip, running his fingers up and down her arm.

Grace smiled slightly. "Of course not. He'd be horrified to know I was here unaccompanied." She dropped her voice. "And I imagine he'd also be horrified to know I'm still being bothered by Drake."

Phillip kissed the top of her head. "Then he'd best not find out about either of these things." He stood, offering her his hand. "Come on. I'll walk you home."

"Ah, Phillip, is that you?" Llewelyn boomed, stepping out of the parlour as Phillip ushered Grace into the house.

Phillip smiled, holding out a hand in greeting. "Good to see you, Mr Dillingham. You look well."

Grace smiled to herself. Her father did look well, she realised. The dark shadows beneath her eyes had faded and his cheeks were pink beneath his beard. She knew it was her own happiness over her upcoming wedding that had caused the change in her father. A part of her regretted not marrying sooner.

"Take that coat off, boy," Llewellyn was saying. "You'll stay for supper. Isn't that right, Gracie?"

Grace smiled at Phillip. "Of course. That would be wonderful." Wonderful, yes, because tonight she would go out into the street and hunt down the patrolling police officers. Point them in Drake's direction. And her story would have far more weight if Phillip was by her side.

She settled Phillip and her father in the parlour with a glass of whisky each and then went to the kitchen to prepare supper.

She could hear the two men chatting amiably across the hall, Llewellyn quizzing Phillip on his business and relaying a humorous story he had heard through a friend.

Grace smiled to herself at their chuckling. It had been far too long since this house had heard laughter. The sound of it warmed her heart.

This was the life she wanted, she thought to herself. A life of caring for the two men she cared about most in the world. A life of listening to them laugh without being weighed down by guilt and regret. And that life was within reach. All she needed was to ensure Drake Matthews never bothered them again.

· · ·

WITH SUPPER FINISHED, Grace ushered Phillip towards the front door. "I'll see Phillip out, Papa." She pulled the front door closed before her father could respond.

The police patrol was due to pass at any moment. Phillip descended the steps at the front of the house and stepped out into the street. He squinted, peering out into the night. The street was empty, save for a fox darting across the road.

"Perhaps we're too early," he said. He put a gentle hand to Grace's shoulder. "You go inside. I'll wait for the patrol."

Grace shook her head. "Here," she said, pointing in the direction of soft, rhythmic footsteps. "Right on time." Two police officers stepped out of the shadows, moving towards the house. Grace hurried towards them with Phillip in tow.

One of the officers bobbed his head in greeting. "Miss Dillingham."

"Our house was defaced again last night," she announced. "And I have reason to believe it was Drake Matthews." Her voice came out brassy and louder than she had intended. The officers eyed each other.

"You're familiar with Mr Matthews, I assume?" said Phillip.

One of the officers gave a slight nod. "We are. And what makes you believe Mr Matthews was involved?"

Grace hesitated. *No proof*, she thought, then shook the thought away. "Mr Matthews was following me yesterday. He threatened me in the street. He's been doing so for years. He blames my father for his father's execution."

"I see," said the officer. For a moment Grace felt foolish. Why had she come to the police? She had nothing on Drake. Nothing but a desperate wish to see him punished for all the dreadful things he had said about her father.

But the officer nodded. "Thank you, Miss Dillingham," he said. "We'll follow up on your concerns."

And then they were off down the street, disappearing around a corner.

Grace let out a breath she hadn't realised she was holding. She turned to look up at Phillip. "Do you think anything will come of it?"

"I don't know," he admitted. "But we've done all we can." He dug his hands into the pockets of his coat. "I'd best be off." He bent to kiss her gently. "Good night, Gracie."

Grace stood on the front steps, waving as

Phillip walked in the opposite direction to the police. She stood for a moment, listening to the stillness of the street. Somewhere in the distance, she heard the rhythmic clatter of horse hooves.

She felt a faint flicker of accomplishment. Perhaps Drake would not be punished. But she had done all she could.

She became dimly aware of murmured voices. Men's voices. Angry, bitter. Growing louder.

Grace raced out into the street and turned the corner. In the orange glow of the streetlamps, she could see Drake and the other men in his gang, striding towards Phillip. Her stomach lurched and she dashed towards them.

Phillip whirled around at the sounds of her footsteps. "Go home, Grace," he told her stiffly. "Everything's all right."

She let out a cold laugh of disbelief; one that was echoed by Drake.

"All right?" he repeated. "You think everything is all right, Butler? After you set the police on me?"

"What else were we to do?" Grace cried before Phillip could speak. "Are we to spend our whole lives being followed and threatened?"

Drake's eyes flashed. "You deserve far worse

than that, Dillingham. You and that murderer of a father of yours."

Phillip stepped in front of Grace before she could retaliate.

"This has to stop, Drake," he hissed. "Your father died more than a decade ago. When are you going to move past it?"

Drake gave a cold laugh. "Move past it?" he repeated. "Is that all my father's life is worth to you? You think I ought to just move past it?" His eyes darted between Phillip and the three members of his gang. "An innocent man was sent to his death."

"Your father was guilty as sin, Drake," Grace cried suddenly, her anger tearing itself free. "He was caught at the church with a ladder in his hand and a pile of lead at his feet." She took a step closer to him, her heart thundering in her chest. Distantly, she heard Phillip say her name, felt his hand against her elbow. But she pulled away, eyes fixed on Drake. "And before he died, he asked my father for a priest so he could confess his sins. Confess to the theft of the lead and other crimes besides."

The moment the words were out of her mouth, Grace regretted them. Llewellyn had told her about Roger Matthews' confession in confidence. He would be horrified to know she had blurted out the information – and to Drake of all people. Still, the words were out, and there was no taking them back. She stared Drake down, eyes flashing. Watched something pass over his eyes. For a fleeting second, he looked rattled and uncertain.

"You're lying," he said darkly.

Grace shook her head. "I'm not lying," she said. "You know I'm not. You know the kind of man your father was."

Drake lurched at her suddenly, but Phillip darted in front of her, nudging her out of Drake's path. Drake shoved hard against Phillip's chest, knocking him to the ground.

Grace heard herself cry out but before she could reach Phillip, he was back on his feet, swinging a wild fist that caught Drake on the side of the jaw.

"Don't you dare touch her," he hissed. "Do you hear me? Just stay the hell away from both of us."

Drake responded with a furious blow of his own, striking Phillip beneath his eye. The three other men advanced at Drake's signal, surrounding Phillip as he fought to keep his balance.

Sickness rose in Grace's throat. These men

were far too strong for Phillip to fight off single-handedly. And this was all her fault. She ought to have kept quiet. Ought to have kept that confidence her father had entrusted her with. She looked back in the direction of the house. Ought she go for her father?

But before she could act, she heard one of Drake's men yell, "Police!"

And they were tearing off into the darkness, leaving Phillip hunched on the side of the road.

PHILLIP LET himself into the house and locked the door behind him. His eye was throbbing and he could feel it beginning to swell. He hurried through the house, checking that every window and door was locked, and drawing the curtains. He hated that he was afraid. But at the back of his mind, he knew Drake Matthews was the kind of man it was wise to fear. A part of him regretted swinging his fists at the man. Another part knew he would do the same again and again. He couldn't bear the thought of him coming after Grace.

With the house secured, Phillip went upstairs to his bedroom and dampened a cloth at the washbasin. He pressed it against his eye and dared to peer in the mirror. His cheek was already cloudy with bruising. He'd be a picture of handsomeness at his wedding that week, he thought wryly. Phillip had been dreaming of marrying Grace for years, and now it was finally a reality, he was to appear at his wedding looking like he'd gone a few rounds in the boxing ring.

After Drake and his gang had disappeared, Grace had ushered him back into her house. She had fussed over his bruised eye and insisted he stay with her and her father that night.

"There's plenty of room for you in the parlour," she had said, a cold cloth pressed to the blooming bruise. "Please don't go back out there. What if Drake and his men are waiting for you?"

Phillip had played down her concerns, assuring her that with the police on alert, Drake and his gang would be long gone.

To allay her fears, he had agreed to take a cab back to his townhouse, despite it being little more than a mile.

He'd believed all he had told Grace and had felt assured of his safety when he'd left the Dillingham's house. But now, with the empty townhouse creaking and groaning around him, and the pain in his eye throbbing in time with his heart, he couldn't help but wish he had taken Grace up on her offer to sleep in their parlour.

He shook the thought away. He was being foolish, he told himself. Letting his imagination run wild. And yet at the back of his mind, he knew his fear was not so foolish. Knew that sending the police after Drake had made him and Grace even more of a target than they had been before.

Exhausted as he was, Phillip's mind was racing and he knew sleep was still hours away. Perhaps he'd make a start on the accounts for the business he had intended to do the next morning.

He carried the lamp down to his study and set it on his desk, tossing a few fresh logs on the fire and stirring it to life. He sat at his desk and pulled the account books from the top drawer. Outside the window, a tree branch tapped against the window, stirred by the cold wind. The fire popped noisily. Phillip peered down at the sums on the page, trying to focus. The numbers seemed to swim in front of his eyes.

A sound outside the window made him look up. The crunch of footsteps?

Perhaps not. Perhaps it was nothing more than

a fox rustling around in the bushes. He dipped his pen in the ink and began to write.

The sound came again, louder this time. Certainly too heavy to be a fox. Phillip paused for a moment, his pen poised, dripping dark beads of ink onto the page. He heard the footsteps move around the side of the house. Heart quickening, Phillip got to his feet and snatched the fire poker from beside the grate. For the first time in his life, he wished he owned a pistol.

With his hand wrapped around the poker, he stepped out into the hallway. Shadows lay thick over the passage, the orange glow of the lamp in the study making dark shapes dance in the doorway.

As he stepped into the kitchen, the window exploded sending glass raining into the kitchen. In leapt Drake Matthews, barely seeming to notice as his coat tore on the sharp teeth of the broken window. His boots thudded loudly against the floor.

Reeling with the shock of it, Phillip held the poker out in front of him. "What the hell do you want, Drake?" he hissed.

Drake stood motionless for a moment, looking Phillip up and down. A smile flickered on the corner of his lips as he took in the rapid swelling of Phillip's eye.

"Thought you'd send the police after me, did you?" he asked, his voice low and dark.

Though his heart was thundering, Phillip held his ground. He would not be intimidated by this man any longer. Enough was enough. He met Drake's eyes, staring him down. His fierce gaze made Phillip's blood chill. Such darkness in his eyes. And at that moment, Phillip knew Drake was capable of anything.

"You hear me, Butler?" Drake spat. "I'm speaking to you."

"Yes, Drake," said Phillip. "I sent the police after you. Because it's time you got out of our lives."

Drake looked taken aback by Phillip's boldness. His lips parted, his heated response falling short. He glanced at the poker Phillip held out in front of him and gave a short, humourless laugh.

"You planning to fight me again, Butler? Didn't go so well for you last time."

Phillip said nothing. Fear prickled the back of his neck. He knew there was every chance Drake carried a pistol in his pocket. Knew there was every chance he would die for this. But he was glad he had found the courage to stand up to this man.

Grace deserved far better than to be harassed by him forever. They both did.

Drake reached into the pocket of his coat and Phillip felt his throat tighten with fear. He gritted his teeth, refusing to let Drake see his terror. He waited for the pistol to appear. Waited for the shot.

Waited to die.

But there was no pistol. Instead, Drake stood for long moments with his hand dug in his pocket, eyes narrowing as he stared at Phillip. Then wordlessly, he turned and climbed back out the window.

His footsteps crunched back around the side of the house before fading away.

Finally, Phillip let himself breathe. He tossed the fire poker to the floor, shaking his cramped fingers. He sank to a chair at the kitchen table and drew in long breaths to steady himself.

A reprieve. But it felt all too fragile. Drake had been seeking revenge since he was eight years old. Phillip knew far better than to imagine this might be the end. But what else was there to do?

He went to the shelf in the kitchen and poured himself a shallow glass of brandy. He tossed it back, staring out the broken window at the black shapes of the garden. Cold wind billowed in through the hole, blowing his hair back from his face and cooling the burn around his eye. The liquor slid hot down his throat, easing his nerves slightly. Then, glass crunching under his boots, he went out to the laundry in search of a cloth to cover the broken window.

## CHAPTER 12

When Phillip appeared at Grace's house that Sunday, his eye was swollen and dark with bruising. Grace let out her breath at the sight of it.

"Oh, Phillip, I'm sorry." She stepped out onto the porch and reached up to stroke his cheek. "I'm sorry," she said. "It was all my fault. I should never have said the things I said to Drake. Does it hurt a lot?"

Phillip shook his head dismissively. "Nothing I can't manage."

Grace gave him a small smile. "I'm sure Drake looks far worse."

Phillip gave a light chuckle. "I hope so."

But beneath his laughter, Grace could hear the strain in his words. She felt it herself; that stab of dread that they might have pushed Drake Matthews too far. She knew he was not the kind of man who would let such a thing slide. He was a dangerous man to have as an enemy.

Phillip looked down at her with a sheepish expression on his face. "Will you still marry me on Friday? Even if I look like I've just stepped out of a boxing ring?"

Grace stood on her tiptoes to kiss him gently. "I'd marry you if you have two black eyes and a bloodied nose." She squeezed his hand. "Especially because I know you did that for me."

Phillip gave her a small smile and then his eyes hardened suddenly. "Was it true what you said the other night?" he asked, his voice low. "About Roger Matthews confessing to his crimes before he died?"

Grace nodded. "Yes. But you're not to repeat it. Papa told me those things in confidence. I'd hate him to know I was unable to keep it a secret."

Phillip nodded. "I'll not tell a soul."

Llewellyn stepped out of the house in his coat and hat, letting out his breath at the sight of

Phillip's eye. "What's all this?" he asked in surprise. "Been starting wars, have you?"

"Phillip's been in the boxing ring," Grace said before Phillip could speak.

"The boxing ring, eh?" said Llewellyn. "Getting rid of a few pre-wedding nerves, are you?"

Phillip smiled slightly. "Something like that."

"And what does Gracie think of all this?" Llewellyn chuckled.

"It's fine, Papa," she said hurriedly, scooping up Phillip's arm and beginning to walk towards the church. "Phillip's already assured me it won't happen again. Now let's go. We're going to be late for the service." She felt hot and flustered and she drew in a long breath to steady herself.

Phillip reached over and wordlessly pressed a hand over hers. Grace managed a small smile, his gentle touch going some way to calm her roiling nerves. She tried to push the thought of Drake from her mind. But the sight of Phillip's swollen eye made it difficult to do.

They turned the corner to approach the church. She had made this walk almost every Sunday for her entire life, Grace realised. And this time next week she would be making a different journey. The next time she walked to the church for the Sunday service, she would be doing so as Phillip's wife.

Despite the bruising on the side of Phillip's face and the churning in her stomach that had not faded since their run-in with Drake and his gang, Grace found herself smiling.

That smile disappeared quickly as they approached the church. Outside the gates stood three policemen, squinting out into the street as though seeking someone out.

Grace frowned, glancing at Phillip and her father. "Why do you suppose they're here? Do you think something has happened?"

Llewellyn shook his head dismissively. "It's all right, Gracie. There's nothing to be concerned about." He chuckled. "You were never one to let the sight of a few police officers unsettle you." He winked at her. "Been up to no good, have you?"

Grace tried to force a smile. But the thought of Phillip and Drake throwing blows in the street was burned into her mind.

As they approached the church gates, the police officers began to stride towards them. Grace felt her heart beat faster. But she kept walking. Her father was right; when had she ever been one to let the sight of a few police officers rattle her? She and Phillip hadn't done a thing wrong. It was Drake who had started the fight.

But when the tallest of the policemen said, "Phillip Butler?" she felt her stomach dive.

Phillip frowned. "Yes, sir?"

"You're under arrest for the murder of William Fenton." Two of the officers grabbed hold of his arms, yanking him free of Grace's grip.

"What?" cried Phillip. "This is ridiculous!"

Grace felt a sudden heat wash over her, her legs suddenly weak. "Murder?" she repeated, the word coming out as little more than a whisper. For a second, the world around her swam and she reached instinctively for her father's broad arm to steady herself.

Phillip spun around to look at her. "This is a mistake, Grace," he said. "I swear it. I never—" His eyes were wide and more fearful than Grace had ever seen them.

"Of course it's a mistake," she managed, her voice wavering. "Let him go!" she demanded. "Phillip would never harm a soul."

One of the officers chuckled. "You sure about that?" He nodded to the bruising on the side of

Phillip's face. "Looks as though he's been seeing a little action."

Grace's breath came hard and fast. "This man, this William Fenton. Who is he?" Her eyes darted between Phillip and the three police officers. Phillip shook his head.

"I've no idea." He struggled against the officers' grip. "This is all a mistake," he hissed. "Let me go."

Grace whirled around to face her father. "Papa! Do something!"

Llewellyn looked squarely at the officers. "This William Fenton. How was he killed? What is Mr Butler being accused of?"

"The victim had multiple knife wounds to the chest," said the officer. "We've two witnesses placing Mr Butler at the scene of the crime."

Grace shook her head in disbelief. "No," she murmured. "No." She hunched over, hit with a sudden sweep of dizziness. Her throat was tight and violent tears threatened to escape. "They're lying!" she cried. "These witnesses, they're lying! Tell them, Phillip!"

But the officers were already hauling him off to the waiting police wagon. "He can tell his story to the magistrate," said one of the officers with a chuckle.

Phillip looked back over his shoulder, catching Grace's eye. But before he could speak again, the officers yanked the back of the wagon open and threw him inside. The policemen leapt into the box seat, the coach disappearing around the corner with the rhythmic clack of hooves against the stone.

Grace stared after it in disbelief. How could this be happening? She and Phillip were to be married in a matter of mere days. Surely she would wake up any second and this would all be some horrible dream. Her tears spilt suddenly, tearing themselves free in loud, racking sobs. She covered her eyes and cried, ignoring the throng of onlookers gathered outside the church.

Her father pulled her into his arms, encircling her in their wide embrace as though he was trying to protect her from the onlookers. Protect her from heartbreak. Protect her from reality.

Distantly, she heard him say, "William Fenton."

She stepped out of his embrace. "You know who he is?"

Llewellyn rubbed his eyes. "William's father was an accomplice of Roger Matthews. It was one of the things Matthews confessed to me before his execution."

Grace let out her breath. "William Fenton was one of Drake's men," she murmured, the sick feeling in her stomach intensifying. "And so were the witnesses, I'm sure of it." She looked up at her father. "Phillip was set up. Drake Matthews did this."

"Drake Matthews?" Llewellyn said finally.

Grace gulped down her tears. "Phillip didn't get that black eye from the boxing ring, Papa. He got it from Drake. They..." Her tears fell harder as she thought back to all she had done. This was all her fault. She had insisted they send the police after Drake. And she had been the one to tell Drake of his father's guilt. She let out another violent sob. "This is all my fault."

Llewellyn gripped her shoulders. "What do you mean, Grace? How is this your fault?"

Between sobs, she told her father about how Drake had followed her home from the seamstress's. About she and Phillip setting out to find the policemen on patrol. About the altercation in the street.

"And then," she coughed, "I told Drake what you told me about Roger Matthews confessing before he was hanged." She swiped at her tears. "I'm so sorry, Papa. I know you told me that in secret. I was just so angry. I'd just had enough of Drake defacing our house, and following me in the street and…" Her words tangled. "All Phillip and I wanted to do was to start our new life together. Have a family of our own. And now I'm so afraid we won't ever…"

Llewellyn pulled her into his arms. "Drake Matthews has been following you?" he asked.

Grace nodded. "He's been bothering the both of us for years, and now…" Her words trailed off in a loud sob.

Llewellyn sighed, tightening his arms around her. "Because of me. Because I was the one to hang Drake's father."

For a long time, Grace didn't speak. "We were to be married," she sobbed. "We were to start our new life. We were going to be so happy."

Llewellyn took a step back, gripping Grace's shoulders and looking her in the eye. "And you still will be, my love. I promise you. I'm going to fix this."

Grace wiped her eyes with the back of her hand. "Fix it?" she repeated. "How?"

"I don't know," Llewellyn admitted. "But I'm going to find a way. I swear it."

Grace nodded, trying to push away the terror

that was lingering at the back of her mind. She needed to believe her father. Needed to believe he would fix this. Needed to believe he would find a way.

The alternative was unbearable.

## CHAPTER 13

For two days after Phillip's arrest, Grace barely moved from her bed. Constant fear pressed down on her and she could hardly bring herself to think about where Phillip was and how he was being treated. On the afternoon of the arrest, she had gone to the police station at Saint James' and demanded to see Phillip. The officer at the front desk had barely looked up from his paperwork before promptly sending her away.

Though her father had forgiven her for sharing the secret he had told her in confidence, Grace couldn't shake the belief that this was all her fault. If only she had just turned her back on Drake as she had done so many times before. If only she had just covered the red paint and not thought twice about it. If only they had done their best to just get on with their lives.

Now she was terrified they would not have the chance. That morning she had found herself cradling the delicate blue folds of her wedding gown, squeezing it to her chest and letting her tears fall into the skirts. How excited she had been for Phillip to see her in this dress. She had stood in front of the mirror at the seamstress's and agonised over every stitch and button. How could such things have felt so important? She would happily marry Phillip in nothing but her undergarments if only they could be safely together.

Her father had done his best to keep her spirits high. Done his best to assure her that justice would prevail and that soon she and Phillip would be beginning their life together just as they had planned. But Grace could see the uncertainty in his eyes. Could hear the thinness of his words. She knew that he feared exactly the same outcome as her.

She and Llewellyn had existed on stale bread and cups of tea for the past two days, and Grace knew that she would have to venture out of the house to the market. She dressed wearily, pushing past the violent ache that urged her to stay hidden beneath her bedclothes.

News of the murder had filtered quickly through the city, Grace realised. As she approached the market, she could hear people talking about the vicious stabbing that had taken place three nights earlier. On a street corner, a newspaper vendor was waving his wares while people gathered around him and murmured to themselves. On the front page of the paper, Grace glimpsed a sketch of Phillip.

She blinked back her tears and put her head down, hurrying away from the newspaper vendor. If the witnesses' stories were to be believed, William Fenton had been attacked from behind while walking home from the Fox and Hound tavern. He had been stabbed with a kitchen knife multiple times and his body left abandoned in the alley.

There was no doubt in Grace's mind that Drake was the true killer. She had no doubt he had taken a knife to one of his own gang members in order to get revenge on her and Phillip. What kind of man was capable of such horrors, she wondered. And Phillip was the one languishing in a prison cell. The one who would face the magistrate in two days. The one who would have to prove himself innocent to avoid the hangman.

Phillip would not be found guilty, she told herself as she paced past the grocer's stall, filling her basket haphazardly. The courts would see that Drake and his men were lying. They would see who the true killer was.

Grace had grown up believing in the courts. The men and women who were sent to her father's scaffold were there because they deserved to be there. The court would not let her down, she told herself.

*It will not let me down.*

As she stood in line at the butcher's stall, she repeated the words over and over in her head, trying desperately to make herself believe them.

"Phillip was transferred to Stepney Prison today," Llewellyn said that night, appearing in the doorway of the kitchen.

Grace looked up at him. He was still dressed in his waistcoat and boots. Shadows of exhaustion underlined his eyes. She could tell he had been sleeping as little as she had.

"Stepney Prison?" she murmured. "I see." She

turned quickly back to the soup pot, tears stinging her eyes. Grace felt as though she had been crying constantly since the moment Phillip had been taken away.

A heavy silence hung over the kitchen. The rest of the words did not need to be said. Phillip had been transferred to the prison where her father was the executioner. If he was found guilty, Llewellyn would be tasked with putting him to death.

Grace's throat tightened. Perhaps it ought to bring her relief, she thought. Her father would never let such a thing happen, surely. After all, he had promised he would fix this. Had promised he would find a way.

But behind her optimism, Grace knew the truth. If Phillip was sent to the gallows at Stepney, Llewellyn would have no choice but to open the trapdoor. At that fleeting moment of execution, the power might have been in his hands but she knew well that her father was as bound by the law as the rest of them.

She dared to look up at him. "Phillip will be found innocent," she squeaked. "Won't he?"

Llewellyn's silence made her throat seize.

"Please, Papa. Promise me he'll be found innocent."

Llewellyn gave her a faint smile, but it didn't reach his eyes. "I hope so."

Grace lifted the soup pot off the range, the smell of it beginning to turn her stomach. "Do you trust the courts, Papa?" she asked.

Llewellyn went to the cupboard and pulled out a fresh bottle of whisky. He pulled out the cork and filled a shallow glass which he emptied in one mouthful. "Yes," he told her. "I do. I have to." He added another glug of liquor to his cup. "I have to believe the men and women sent to me are guilty. How could I do my job otherwise?"

But Grace could hear the uncertainty in his words.

WHEN GRACE WOKE on the morning of Phillip's trial, it was still dark. Her entire body was aching with exhaustion. She had not managed more than a few stilted hours of sleep all night. In truth, she had managed little more than stilted sleep since the dreadful day the police had appeared outside the church and carted Phillip off to the police wagon.

Tonight, everything would be all right, she told herself. Tonight, the world would know that Phillip was innocent. Would know that Drake Matthews and his men were the ones who deserved to face the hangman. And when her father opened the trapdoor beneath Drake, Grace would be there in the execution yard watching him fall.

She emptied a jug of water into her washbasin and splashed her face, trying to wash away her exhaustion. Then she combed and pinned her hair neatly and buttoned herself into a neat grey dress. She wanted to make herself as presentable as possible. She wanted the magistrate to see her and think, *well that Phillip Butler cannot be guilty. He is betrothed to such a fine young woman...*

She peered at her reflection in the mirror. Her eyes were cloudy and swollen with the tears that had not left her in days. Her skin was pale and drawn. But her blonde hair was pinned in a neat knot at her neck, and her skirts were clean and pressed. Presentable, she thought, if only just.

Llewellyn rode with her to the courthouse. They sat wordlessly in the coach, Grace's hands knotted tightly in her lap. She stared out the window. The morning was grey and overcast, a heavy gloom pressing down upon the city. It did little to help the nerves that were roiling inside her.

They were led into the courtroom and sat side by side on the bench in the front row. On the periphery of her vision, Grace could see two of Drake's men – men she remembered from Hyde Park. Men who had attacked Phillip in the street outside her house. Did they know the truth, she wondered. Did they know Drake had murdered one of their own to get his twisted revenge? And then a worse thought came to her. Were these the men who had claimed to have witnessed Phillip commit the crime? Had they had a part in the murder themselves? She turned away, forcing herself not to look at them. She refused to give them the satisfaction of knowing just how much they scared her. She closed her eyes for a second, forcing her hatred back down.

But she could feel the men's presence. Was acutely aware of them on the edge of her vision, murmuring to each other, turning their eyes towards her. And when she heard sharp footsteps clicking towards them, she knew without turning around that those footsteps belonged to Drake.

She felt her breathing quicken. Felt her father press a steadying hand to her shoulder.

"It's all right, Gracie," he murmured. "Don't even look at him."

Grace gritted her teeth. Clenched her hand into an angry fist. And she kept her eyes forward, avoiding even a glimpse at Drake.

The door at the back of the courtroom creaked and out came Phillip, a policeman holding each of his arms. Phillip was wearing a ragged shirt and grimy trousers and wore thick sand-coloured stubble on his jaw. His bruised eye was still swollen and discoloured, and there was a fresh cut on his other cheek.

Grace felt tears behind her eyes. She had no doubt the police officers had given him the cut. Her stomach turned over at the thought of him being mistreated.

Phillip turned slightly, catching her eye. Grace forced a smile, trying to force down her tears. She needed Phillip to be calm and level-headed. She needed him to tell the magistrate his story, tell him of his innocence. And then the truth would be known.

Phillip attempted a smile of his own but Grace could see the fear in his eyes.

Her father reached over and gave her hand a reassuring squeeze.

Phillip was led to the dock, and his charges were read out.

*Murder of William Fenton.*

As Grace had feared, the first person called to the stand was one of Drake's men who had watched her enter the courtroom. The young man was broad-shouldered and unshaven; hard, dark eyes shining above the chaotic mess of his beard.

"Please tell the court what you witnessed on the evening of the twelfth of August."

For a moment, the witness's eyes fell to Phillip and then shifted across the courtroom to Grace. She felt the muscles in her shoulders tighten with a dizzying mix of anger and fear.

"The two of us left the Fox and Hound Tavern around midnight," he began, voice as rough and cold as Grace had imagined it to be. As I was leaving, I heard a commotion in the alley behind the building."

"What kind of commotion?"

"Shouting. Men arguing."

"What did you do?"

"I followed the sound. Found William Fenton

arguing with Mr Butler. Will had left the tavern a few minutes before I had."

"What were the men arguing about?"

"I don't know. I couldn't make it out. But the next thing I knew, Mr Butler had pulled a knife. Stabbed Will with it four or five times." He fixed his dark glare on Phillip. "I went after him, but the coward ran off before I could get there. Poor Will were already dead."

A murmur went through the courtroom.

"He's lying," Grace hissed. "How can no one see that?"

Llewellyn squeezed her wrist to calm her.

The second witness's story was identical. The two men had left the tavern to come upon Phillip fighting with William Fenton in the alley. They had witnessed the stabbing but had been too late to save their friend.

As the second witness garbled through his lies, Grace let her gaze fall to Phillip. Kind, gentle Phillip; that timid little boy who had feared their schoolmaster back when they were children. How could anyone believe him capable of such a horrifying act?

Finally, Phillip was brought to the stand. Grace's heart was thundering, her skin damp with sweat beneath her shift. Surely when Phillip spoke, the court would see the character of man he truly was. Surely they would see him incapable of doing the things he had been accused of. They had to. There could be no other way.

As Phillip swore upon the bible, his voice was low and thin. Grace could hear the fear in his words. She tried to meet his eye, tried to assure him that everything would be all right. If only he could show the court who he really was.

Show the court who Drake Matthews really was.

The magistrate rattled through his questions in a cold, monotonous voice.

"Where were you on the night of the twelfth of August?"

"How did you come to know William Fenton?"

"What were you arguing about?"

And although Phillip spoke calmly and slowly, his words were thin and his voice trembled slightly.

*I was at home on the night of the twelfth. Yes, I was alone. My daily had left earlier in the evening.*

*I've never met William Fenton in my life.*

And up to the stand came false witness after false witness; men who claimed to have seen

Phillip drinking at the Fox and Hound Tavern on the night of Fenton's murder. Men who had claimed to have seen the men arguing. Claimed to have seen Phillip following Fenton into the street.

Where had all these witnesses come from, Grace wondered sickly. Were they men from Drake's gang? Or were they mere passers-by who had been threatened by Drake into speaking out against Phillip?

Out of the corner of her eye, she could see a smile on the faces of the two men who had first taken the witness stand. And as she turned to glare at them, Grace's eyes met Drake's. Unlike the other men, he offered her no hint of a smile. He just stared at her with the same dark glare she had seen from him when he had first accused Llewellyn of murdering his father. The same glare that had haunted her for the past ten years. Suddenly, something tore open inside her. She leapt suddenly to her feet. "These men are lying!" she cried. "Can't you see that!"

Llewellyn reached for her hand and tried to tug her back down. "Sit down, Grace," he murmured. She pulled away sharply and pointed a wild finger at Drake.

"He was the one who did this. He was the one

who killed his friend. To punish us. To get his miserable revenge! He's an animal! He's the one who deserves to die!"

The magistrate turned to one of the policemen flanking the crowd. "Please remove her from the courtroom."

The policeman was upon her in a second, grabbing her arms in a tight vice-like grip and hauling out from the bench.

"Let go of me!" she cried. She was dimly aware of her father on the other side of her, taking her other arm gently as the policeman herded her towards the door.

Grace turned back to look at Phillip. His eyes were wide, filled with terror, mouthing words to her she couldn't make out. And then her eyes fell to the magistrate as he reached beneath the desk and produced a black cap.

Grace heard herself cry out at the sight of it. Her legs gave way beneath her as the policeman shoved her out into the passage behind the courtroom.

Phillip was destined for the hangman.

# CHAPTER 14

Grace rode back home in a daze. She was dimly aware of her father in the carriage beside her, dimly aware of the coach rattling over the road. But her eyes were glazed, her vision swimming. All she could fathom was that Phillip was to die.

Kind, gentle Phillip, who had never hurt a soul in his life.

Silent tears streamed down her face. She felt trapped in the worst nightmare possible.

"Grace?" Her father's gentle voice cut through her thoughts. "We're here." She let him take her hand and lead her out of the carriage. Let him unlock the door and usher her inside. Let him take her to the armchair in the parlour.

She stared into the unlit grate. How was she to go on? How was she to live in a world in which there were so many injustices? How was she to live in a world without the man she loved?

And how was she to live when she had this horrid, burning anger directed at Drake and his men simmering inside her?

"Here." Her father handed her a steaming cup of tea.

Grace stared down at the cup in disinterest.

"Drink it," said Llewellyn. "It will help." Grace could hear the unsteadiness in his voice. He sounded drained and broken. She brought the cup to her lips and took a small sip.

The tea did nothing to steady her or calm her racing thoughts. All it did was turn her stomach. She set the cup on the side table and fixed her gaze back on the cold fireplace.

The armchair beside her squeaked as her father sank into it.

Her father who was to end the life of the man she loved.

The thought caused a fresh sob to escape her. She pressed a hand hard against her eyes, trying to will herself away.

"Oh, Gracie," sighed Llewellyn. "I wish there was something I could do."

Grace looked up at him. "There must be," she said. "There must. Please, Papa. You have to find a way to save him."

But even as she spoke, she knew there was no chance. She knew better than anyone that her father had no control over the people he put to death. She thought about the mother and daughters executed for murder. Thought about the young man who had stolen to feed his family. She had seen the toll this job had taken on him. And she knew without a doubt that none of the executions he had performed in the past would be quite as unbearable for either of them as this one.

EVERY DAY her father left for work that week, Grace felt herself turning away, unable to watch him leave. In four days he would be stepping out that door to hang Phillip. Three days. Two days... She felt so utterly helpless as the days and then the hours slipped away.

With each passing minute, Phillip's moment of death grew nearer. Soon she would have to exist in a world without him. Meanwhile, Drake and his men would have the run of the city, carrying on with their lives as though nothing had happened.

She couldn't bear to think about that future. How bleak the world would be without Phillip.

She threw herself into the housework, scrubbing and polishing every inch of the house, mending clothing that didn't need mending, baking more loaves of bread than she and Llewellyn could ever eat. Anything to keep her mind from dwelling on the reality.

She had seen little of her father over the past few days. Grace wondered if it was guilt that was keeping him from her.

She thought of all the time he had spent in the taverns and gambling halls after she had caught him selling the young woman's body. She couldn't bear for him to fall into his old habits again. Not now that she needed him so desperately. All these empty hours alone at the house felt almost unendurable.

But a part of her understood her father's distance. How could he look her in the eye, given what he was about to do?

How would things be between them after Phillip's execution? Though Grace knew, of course, that her father had no choice in the matter, a part of her was afraid of what it might do to their fragile relationship. Would she think of Phillip every time she looked at her father? Would she always look upon him as the man who had killed her beloved?

She shook the thought away. It was not her father who would bring about Phillip's death. It was Drake Matthews. He was responsible for Phillip's impending death as surely as if he had fired a pistol into his chest. And bubbling up inside her, she realised with a dark sense of dread, was her own desperate need for revenge.

GRACE WAITED until the house was still. She could hear her father's soft snoring coming from the room beside her own. It had taken him hours to fall asleep.

Soundlessly, she slid out of bed and pulled on her dress and boots. She crept down the stairs, each step carefully placed to avoid making a sound.

She stepped out into an eerily quiet street. She could hear not a sound from the city; not the rattle of wheels or hooves, not a single voice or footstep.

Grace realised she had never been outside so late before.

Before her nerves could get the better of her, she began to walk.

She had only a dim thought of how to find the Fox and Hound Tavern. All she knew about the place she had learned during Phillip's trial. And she had no clue whether she would find Drake and his men there. But she could think of nowhere else to look.

She stood for several moments outside the tavern, staring through the grimy windows into the dim, lamplit interior. The place was quiet with just a few clusters of men in each corner of the bar. Before she could change her mind, she pushed the door open.

Several heads turned as she strode inside. And in a corner was Drake, sitting at a table with several of the men she recognised from the trial. He put down his glass of ale and got to his feet, pacing slowly towards her.

Grace was dimly aware she ought to have been afraid. But all she felt was hatred.

"Well now," said Drake, his boots thudding rhythmically against the stone floor. "If it ain't

Grace Dillingham. Didn't imagine I'd see a fine upstanding lass like you in a place like this."

Grace gritted her teeth. She regretted coming. But it was far too late for regret. Before she knew what she was doing, she was charging at Drake, swinging wild fists into his chest. She heard the men around him break into laughter.

"You're an animal!" she cried. "How could you do that to Phillip? And how could you do that to one of your own men?" Tears flooded her cheeks.

Drake gripped her shoulder roughly, forcing her backwards. The shock of it caused Grace to swallow her tears. Drake shoved her towards the door and out into the street, shoving her to her knees outside the tavern. Drake's men surrounded her. Which one of these men had been the one to kill William Fenton, Grace wondered sickly. Would they kill her too? She didn't care. How could she value her life when she was to live without the man she loved?

She scrambled to her feet as Drake advanced on her, his stale breath hot against her cheek. "Keep your damn mouth shut," he hissed. "Or yours'll be the next body they find in that alley."

Grace glared at him, daring him. "One day

you're going to get what you deserve, Drake," she hissed.

He chuckled. "Is that why you came, Dillingham? To give me a warning?"

Grace said nothing. Why had she come? Nothing she did would scare a man like Drake Matthews, of course. But she had wanted him to see this new fearlessness in her, wrought by Phillip's approaching death. She wanted him to see that she was no longer that scared little girl running from him in the schoolyard.

"Grace?" She whirled around, surprised to hear her father's voice. Llewellyn was charging down the street towards her and the men, eyes full of fear. He had thrown his trousers and coat on over his nightshirt, she realised. A pang of regret hit her. She'd assumed her father had been asleep when she had left the house. She'd had no thought he'd been following her.

But she also realised she was glad to see him. Not just for the faint hint of security his presence offered but because she wanted Drake to see them together. Perhaps this was the other reason she had hunted Drake down in the middle of the night. To show him she was proud of her father. To show him all the cruel words he had spouted about

Llewellyn Dillingham over the years had not made her see him in a different light.

*Murderer,* Drake could say, over and over again.

*Burn in hell.*

But none of that would change the fact that deep down Grace knew her father was inherently good.

Even if he was to end the life of the man she loved.

Llewellyn thundered up the empty street, clutching Grace's arm and stepping in front of her to shield her from Drake and his men. He turned to look at his daughter.

"What on earth are you doing out here, Grace?" She could see the terror in his eyes. "Did these men—"

"Well, if it ain't the hangman himself," Drake drawled. He stepped forward shoving Llewellyn hard against the chest. "How do you sleep at night, Dillingham?"

"How dare you lay a hand on my father!" Grace cried, trying to push past Llewellyn to get to Drake. Her father held out a broad arm, preventing her from passing.

"Gracie," he murmured. He turned back to

Drake. "Perhaps you ought to ask yourself the same question."

Drake reached into his pocket and slid out a pistol. Grace's heart leapt into her throat. And at once she saw the utter foolishness of coming out here. She ought to have known her father would come after her. And now she had led Drake directly to the man he despised. She knew he would have no hesitation in pulling the trigger.

"No," she heard herself cough. "Please."

How could she lose her father when she was to lose Phillip?

Drake stood with the pistol held out in front of him, barrel aimed squarely at Llewellyn's chest. Around him, his men were silent; watching, waiting.

"Do you really want to kill me, Drake?" Llewellyn asked, with a quiet, eerie calmness. "Do you really think you'll get away with another murder?" He nodded back towards the tavern. "There are plenty of people inside. Do you think they'll all stay quiet? Or will you pay them off again like you did those sham witnesses at Phillip Butler's trial?"

Despite the situation, Grace felt a tiny flicker of satisfaction that her father had dared voice the obvious. She watched something pass over Drake's eyes. Surprise that someone had dared call him out on all the dreadful things he had done. Especially when he was standing on the wrong end of a pistol.

"Wouldn't you rather let me suffer, Drake?" Llewellyn continued. "Why would you put me out of my misery?"

Drake faltered. Grace could tell her father's reaction was one he had not been expecting.

Finally, Drake lowered the pistol. "You're right," he hissed. "Death is far too easy for you. You should suffer. How could I end your life when you've got such important things to do such as putting Phillip Butler to death?"

Grace's anger flared suddenly and she lurched wildly at Drake. Before she could reach him, Llewellyn's broad arms circled her, pulling her away. Her father held her tightly, preventing her from moving as Drake and his men turned and disappeared back inside the tavern.

Finally, Llewellyn released his grip, his breathing loud and strained.

Grace burst into tears. "I'm sorry, Papa. I'm so sorry. I just wanted to…" She faded out. All the reasons she had found for charging after Drake in the night suddenly seemed so foolish. Nothing she did tonight would have changed anything for Phillip. And she had almost lost her father in the process.

Llewellyn wrapped his arms around her again, letting her sob into his broad chest. He didn't speak, as though he knew nothing he said could take away her pain. But Grace was just glad for his presence. Glad for someone to cling to as her world fell around her.

## CHAPTER 15

"*P*apa," said Grace the next morning, "will you take me to see Phillip?" Her eyes filled with tears as she spoke. "To say goodbye?" She hunched at one end of the kitchen table, hands wrapped around a mug of tea that had long gone cold.

The following day, Phillip was to be put to death. A sense of bitter resignation had fallen over Grace. She knew nothing she did, nothing her father did, could save Phillip now.

For several moments, Llewellyn didn't speak. He just sawed away at the stale remains of a bread loaf sitting on the table. Surely he would not deny her this, Grace thought. Surely he would allow her to say farewell to the man she loved.

His hesitation, she knew, did not come from his need to adhere to any law. Grace knew as well as anyone that prisoners at Stepney were permitted visitors. And since the death of Phillip's father, she was all he had. She would not let him go to his death without anyone saying goodbye.

But before she could open her mouth to voice these thoughts, her father nodded.

"If you're certain."

"Of course I am."

Llewellyn put down the bread knife, discarding his attempts at breakfast. "Put your shoes on," he said distantly. "I'm to leave in a few minutes."

Stepney Prison had never felt more bleak or foreboding. And Grace's heart had never beat as hard as it was at that moment as her father led her down the gloomy passage to Phillip's cell.

Tears stung her eyes, and she forced them away. She didn't want to appear at Phillip's door as a tearful mess. She wanted to show at least a faint flicker of strength. She needed to show him she would be all right on her own. Show him she would manage to survive once he was gone. Even if she was not certain that was the case.

But the moment the guard opened the door, the tears she had been holding back spilt. Grace rushed into Phillip's cell, throwing her arms around him. He wrapped his arms around her, pulling her into him. His entire body felt cold. She clung harder, trying to warm him. Finally, he took a step back, gripping the tops of her arms, his face close to hers.

For a long time neither spoke, just stared into each other's eyes. Grace's chest was aching, tears sliding silently down her cheeks. She thought of all the plans for their life they had made; the children they would have, the growth of his business, what colour they would paint each room of the townhouse. And for all their planning, their work, their wishing, Phillip was to spend his last hours in this dank and lightless cell, dressed in stained and torn clothing, the stench of human waste hanging in the air.

He pressed his palm to her cheek. "I want you to carry on living your life, Grace," he said firmly. "Promise me. You're not to mourn me forever. You're to find someone else who will make you happy. Who'll give you the life you deserve."

His words made fresh tears spill down Grace's cheeks. She threw herself back into his arms, burying her head against his chest. "No," she sobbed. "Never. I love you."

"I love you too, Grace," said Phillip, his voice wavering. "More than anything else in the world. And that's why—" He swallowed heavily, his words caught in his throat. "And that's why I need you to promise me this."

Grace clung to fistfuls of his shirt. How could she make such a promise? The thought of ever moving out from beneath this violent grief was unimaginable, let alone finding someone to take Phillip's place. But if this promise would make it even an ounce easier for Phillip to walk to the gallows, then it was a promise she would make.

She managed a tiny nod. "Yes, Phillip," she murmured. "I promise."

"Good." He held his lips to the top of her head.

The guard rapped loudly on the door. "Time."

"No," Grace sobbed. "No, no, no." She clung tightly to Phillip, trying to memorise every inch of him. When she finally tore herself away, his eyes were glistening. He held his lips to hers and Grace felt tears slide down his cheeks, mingling with her own.

"Be strong, Gracie," he said. "I love you."

"I love you too," she told him again. "I always will."

The guard marched into the cell. "That's time, Miss Dillingham," he barked. He made to grab for her arm but she pulled away. And against the urging of every muscle in her body, she turned away from Phillip and walked out of the cell.

THAT NIGHT, Grace didn't sleep. How could she, given what was to come the next day? How could she sleep away any of these last precious moments in which Phillip Butler was part of the world? A part of her felt as though she were the one about to face the gallows.

She thought of the condemned cell at Stepney Prison; a place she had come to know far too well over the past years. The thought of Phillip in there made her ache. Was he sleeping, she wondered. Or was he too lying awake in the darkness, his thoughts racing faster than he ever imagined possible. Was he lying there in fear, terrified of what was to come?

Her father would ensure he was calm, she told herself. Her father always made sure people went to their deaths with dignity. But would he be able to do so when Phillip was the man walking towards the scaffold?

The first hint of morning light filtered through the curtains, making fresh tears prick her eyes. Would it be like this forever, she wondered. Would she collapse into tears at every fleeting thought of her lost love?

She wiped her eyes hard as though trying to force the tears away. She couldn't fall apart right now. Not today. Phillip had to go to his death calmly, with dignity. And she would not help the situation if she was on her knees in the execution yard, sobbing violently. Today she would be strong for Phillip.

And once he was gone, she would allow herself to fall apart.

As she splashed her face at the washbasin, she told herself again.

*Today I will be strong for Phillip.*

She climbed into her dress, fastening the hooks with shaky fingers.

But she would not fall apart.

*Today I will be strong.*

When she climbed downstairs to heat the kettle, her father was already in the kitchen. He frowned at the sight of her. "Go back upstairs,

Grace. I don't want you there today. It's best you stay here."

Grace stared at him in disbelief. "Stay here? No!"

Llewellyn gripped her shoulders. "Please, Grace. I couldn't bear for you to witness…" He trailed off. And she realised then that he did not just want her to stay away for her own sake. He couldn't bear for her to watch him open the trapdoor beneath the man she loved.

"Papa…" she began, her words fading away. She wanted to tell him that she would not blame him. Would not hold it against him. Wanted to tell him that she understood the guilt roiling inside him. But she knew if she spoke of those things, the tears she was trying so hard to hold back would escape down her cheeks. And that she could not allow.

*Today I will be strong…*

Instead, she just looked up at her father. "I have to be there," she said, forcing herself to keep her voice level. "I can't let Phillip go to the gallows on his own."

Her father sighed. "Are you certain?"

"Of course." Her voice wavered, but she held Llewellyn's gaze.

"All right," he said finally. "I can't stop you. But

you're to go straight to the public viewing yard. You're not to come inside with me." His voice was thin.

Grace swallowed hard. She nodded. For the best, she told herself. She could not bring herself to see Phillip in the condemned cell. The sight of it would destroy her.

GRACE STOOD at the back of the execution yard, her spine pressed against the stone wall to keep herself from falling. Bright sunlight streamed into the yard, the sky overhead was almost violently blue.

This wasn't right. How could the sun be shining on the day Phillip was to die?

The execution yard was slowly filling with people. Though her father's executions never drew as many viewers as Calcraft's tasteless theatrics, plenty of people, it seemed, were coming to view the demise of the city's latest convicted killer. The man who had so viciously taken a life outside the Fox and Hound Tavern.

Grace hated that this was how Phillip would be remembered. That this was what the world saw when they looked at the man she adored. She was glad Phillip's father was not here to witness this horror.

Around her, people were chatting loudly, bursts of laughter hanging in the air. Grace clenched her hands into fists. How dare they laugh? What could possibly be so amusing at a time like this?

She closed her eyes and tried to will herself away. Her legs felt as though they would give way at any point. She fought the urge to turn around and race out of the jail yard. She gripped tight fistfuls of her skirts, trying to conjure up a little strength. Trying to stop herself from collapsing.

The door to the prison opened, and Grace heard a soft cry of horror escape her. This was it. This was the moment she had been dreading since the policemen had first marched towards Phillip outside the church two weeks ago. There had been a tiny part that had believed this horror might never come. A tiny part that refused to believe the world could be so cruel. But here was her father, hidden in his hood, his gaze fixed on the noose directly ahead of him. He climbed the steps to the scaffold.

The murmuring of the crowd had vanished, to be replaced by a thick, weighty silence. Grace pushed her way towards the front of the crowd.

She needed Phillip to see her. Needed him to know that he was not alone.

But when Phillip appeared in the doorway, the black hood was already pulled down low. With a hand on each of his arms, the guards led him onto the scaffold. Grace felt her tears threatening. She had hoped for one last glimpse at the face of the man she loved. Hoped she might have the chance to look him in the eyes and let her look convey how much she would miss him.

Perhaps it was for the best, she told herself. She did not want her last memory of Phillip to be the fear in his eyes as he prepared to lose his life. She wanted to remember only the good times; their first kiss by the fire, walks by the Serpentine, rowing on the lake at the Pleasure Gardens.

Grace felt sickness rise in her throat as her father placed the noose around Phillip's head. They were both calm, she noticed distantly. Both carrying themselves with dignity. But it did nothing to ease the grief and terror that was pressing down on her.

She felt hot and dizzy. Forced herself to swallow again and again to keep the sickness down. She wanted to scream, wanted to race onto the scaffold herself and stop this from happening.

But she did none of that. Her legs felt weighted and her mouth too dry to even make a sound. A deep trembling took over her entire body.

In a second, it was over; the trapdoor opened and Phillip's body disappeared beneath the scaffold. Grace was dimly aware of her father turning to look her way.

She heard herself cry out. Her tears spilt suddenly and her legs, which moments earlier had refused to move an inch, were now desperate to escape this place. She whirled around, shoving past the people behind her in a frantic attempt to find the gate. She raced out of the prison yard and collapsed to her knees in the street.

## CHAPTER 16

*G*race stayed hunched against the wall of the prison for several long moments, hugging her knees to her chest and coughing down a violent rush of tears. Around her, she could hear footsteps and voices and the crowd filtering out of the prison yard. The clop of hooves sounded up and down the road, and two young girls laughed as they rolled a hoop along the street. All around her, life was carrying on as it always had.

How could that be possible? Things would never be the same again.

She kept her eyes pressed hard against her knees. How was she to carry on with her life now that Phillip was gone? How could she ever move past this, the way she had promised Phillip she would?

Then a sudden thought seized her. Her father would come looking for her. No doubt he had seen her tear out of the execution yard. She was certain he would soon come to try and offer her a little comfort.

The thought made her climb to her feet. She couldn't face her father right now. Over and over she had told herself she would not hold it against him that he had been the one to kill her beloved. And yet now all she could feel was a bitter resentment welling up inside. her.

She needed to leave. Right now, before her father found her.

Grace had only dull recollections of getting home. She had hailed a cab, she supposed, although she remembered little of the journey. All she knew was that now she was standing in front of the house, staring at the front door which hung wide open.

Her first thought was that Drake and his gang had paid her a visit. But as she walked shakily up the front steps, she realised that was not the case.

She could hear a voice echoing through the house; one man shouting orders at another.

"Careful of the wall! Turn it on its side."

The two men strode down the hallway, carrying the kitchen table.

"What are you doing?" Grace cried. "Put that down at once!"

One of the men glanced over his shoulder at her. The other did not even flinch. They marched past her and down the front steps, hauling the table into the back of a large wagon parked outside the house. In her daze, Grace had not even noticed it when she arrived home.

She chased the men out into the street. In the back of the wagon, she could see other pieces of their belongings: the side table from the parlour and all four kitchen chairs.

"What are you doing?" she cried again. "Those things belong to us!"

"Not any more they don't. They've been sold."

"Sold? What do you mean they've been sold? To who?"

The men didn't answer; just marched back towards the house with Grace hurrying after them. They went to the parlour and lifted her father's favourite armchair. Grace blocked their way, arms across the doorway to prevent them from leaving.

"Put that down!" she cried. "That's my father's! He would never sell that!"

The first man nodded for the younger one to put the chair down. He sighed heavily and reached into his pocket, holding a piece of paper out to Grace.

"Here," he said gruffly. "It's all here. Your father was the one who sent us. Told us to get rid of the lot."

Grace snatched the page from his hand and skimmed over it. Almost every item of furniture in the house was listed on the page, along with the sum to be paid for each piece. And sure enough, there was her father's signature, scrawled at the bottom of the document.

Her eyes darted from the page to the half-empty parlour. Why would her father do this? Had she not done a good enough job handling their money? Was his gambling worse than she realised? Was he selling all their furniture to keep the debt collectors away?

The older man grabbed the page and shoved it back in his pocket. "May we get by?" he asked pointedly.

Without speaking, Grace stepped aside, her eyes fixed to the blank square of floor where her father's favourite armchair had stood for as long as she could remember.

BY THE TIME the men left, the house was little more than an empty shell. The parlour was bare and all that remained in the kitchen was the range and a few blackened pots. Even the beds had been taken, leaving Grace and Llewellyn to sleep on thin mattresses on the floor.

Unsure what else to do, Grace sat on the floor of the parlour, her back pressed to the bare wall. She hugged her knees, eyes glazed over. She couldn't make sense of any of this.

At the sound of a key in the door, Grace leapt to her feet and rushed into the hallway.

"Papa!" she demanded. "These men, they took all the furniture! Did you send them?"

Llewellyn stepped past her wearily. He took off his hat and coat and hung them on the hook beside the door.

"Yes, Grace," he said flatly, pacing into the kitchen. "I sent them." There was a heaviness about her father, Grace noticed. His shoulders were slumped and his eyes dull and lifeless.

She grabbed his arm, forcing him to face her. "Why? What's this about, Papa? Do you have more gambling debts that I don't know about?"

Llewellyn didn't speak at once. He peered into Grace's eyes, and in his gaze she saw remorse and pain. "Debts," he said finally. "Yes, Grace, I have debts. Debts I can never repay."

Grace frowned. "What do you mean?"

Llewellyn shook his head. "I'm sorry, Gracie. I'm sorry for everything." He glanced around the empty kitchen and then stepped past her again, disappearing up the stairs to his bedroom with slow, heavy steps.

GRACE HEARD nothing more from her father that night. A part of her was hot with resentment. How could her father sell all their belongings and then offer barely an explanation? Leave her alone in an empty house tonight of all nights? But another part of her was glad for his distance. As much as she wanted an explanation for this stripped-bare house, she was not sure she could face her father without seeing him open the trapdoor beneath Phillip.

Unable to stomach supper, Grace returned to the floor of the parlour with a teacup in her hands. Alone in the empty room, her thoughts drifted back to her childhood. She thought of sitting beside the fire with her parents, listening to her mother's laughter, seeing the love in her father's eyes as he smiled at his wife.

How distant that time seemed. How had things changed so much? The death of her baby sister, she thought, was when things had begun to turn. Was when the happiness had begun to drain so quickly from her mother.

But Grace knew it about far more than that. So much of her mother's melancholy, she knew, had been as a result of Llewellyn's job. Her mother had hated the gossip and the insults hurled in the street. Hated the stripes of red paint that appeared so often on their front door. Her father's job, in its own twisted way, had taken Veronica from them.

And now Grace could feel her relationship with Llewellyn dangling by a thread. Over and over she had told herself she would not hold her father responsible for Phillip's death. But now it had happened and she couldn't help but feel a cold resentment for the man who had placed the noose around his neck. The man who had opened the trapdoor. She was not sure she would ever be able to look her father in the eye again.

Grief pressed down on her. Raw, agonising grief over Phillip and a dull and bitter ache stirred up the thought of her mother. At her resentment towards her father. She felt as hollow and empty as the rooms around her. Too exhausted, too drained to move, she curled up into a ball and fell asleep on the bare parlour floor.

SHE WOKE to the sound of the front door slamming shut. Pale morning light spilt into the room through curtains she had not bothered closing the night before. A cold cup of tea sat untouched beside her head. For a moment, Grace felt disoriented. Where was she? Why was the parlour empty? But memories of the previous day swung back at her violently, causing her to let out a soft murmur of grief.

She climbed shakily to her feet and went to the window, catching sight of her father disappearing around the corner.

Grace stared after him. Phillip was to be buried

today, she knew. How could her father have simply left her alone on such a day, without so much as a word to see how she was faring? Perhaps he could sense that Grace was holding him responsible despite her best efforts not to do so. But despite the resentment she felt, she needed him. She couldn't bear to be alone on a day like this. Llewellyn was all she had in the world now. How could her father not understand how much she needed him? Take him out of her life and she had nothing.

Grace took her cloak from the hook above the door and slid it on, not bothering with breakfast or even a cup of tea. All she cared about was getting to the prison in time for Phillip's burial. She knew there would be no one else there to mourn him. After his father had died, there had been no one else left in his family. His friends and clients had turned away after the murder. Grace wondered if they truly believed him guilty or whether they were simply distancing themselves from the whole affair. What a cruel injustice it was that Phillip would even be robbed of the chance of being buried beside his beloved family. Instead, he was to spend eternity in the burial yard of a prison, surrounded by killers and thieves. Meanwhile, Drake Matthews was to roam free.

Grace climbed from the cab outside Stepney Prison. It was a journey that was becoming far too familiar. A journey, she knew instinctively, she would never make again after today. She thought of all the occasions she had come here to help her father; of the three women she had helped go calmly to their deaths. Of all the days she had met him outside the prison gates so that he might not be alone on his way home from work.

She climbed from the cab and stared up at the building, bitter hatred for the place welling up inside her. At that moment it felt as though the place was a symbol of all that was wrong with the world.

Since the days she had first started to understand it, she had never agreed with the practice of putting men and women to death. And yet she had kept coming back over and over again. Countless times she had walked those passages, following the footsteps of prisoners whose lives were about to end. A testament, Grace supposed, of how much she had loved her father.

But she would not come here ever again. How could she, now that it carried such dreadful memories? Phillip was to be buried here, yes, but this was not where she would come to remember him. She would do that in places where they had shared joyful times: the Pleasure Gardens in Vauxhall; their favourite wooden bench beside the Serpentine. At the thought, fresh tears welled up inside her and cascaded down her cheeks.

Letting them fall freely, she trudged past the main entrance of the jail to the side gate she knew led to the burial yard. Her father had left the house so hurriedly he would have no thought that she was here, but she supposed if she waited by the gate, surely he might see her and allow her into the grounds for the burial.

But as she turned the corner, Grace stopped walking. A carriage stood outside the gate, a large black horse standing patiently in front of it. That coach, she knew it well. She had seen its dark wheels and panels many nights in her dreams. It belonged to the anatomist's assistant – the man who had paid her father to take the body of the young woman hanged for murder a little more than a year ago. And there, in the thick shadow of the jail, stood her father, head lowered, deep in conversation with the coachman.

She stared in disbelief. Surely this what not what it looked like. Phillip had been the only person hanged at Stepney Prisoner yesterday. His was the only body to be buried today.

Grace felt hot and then cold. She felt unable to move, seized with anger, with hatred, with unbearable grief.

*He wouldn't*, she told herself. *He couldn't.*

Surely.

But then she thought of the empty house. Of the way in which the two men had carted all their furniture into their wagon. She thought of the ledger the man had pushed into her hand, proving it had been her father's choice to sell everything they owned.

There were money problems. There had to be. And with every piece of furniture sold, Llewellyn had no choice left but to sell Phillip's body.

Sudden anger overtaking her and Grace broke into a run, but before she could reach the carriage, her father and the anatomist's assistant disappeared into the jail. Moments later, they returned to the gate carrying a body wrapped in a colourless cloth. At the sight of it, fresh tears stung Grace's eyes. Tears of grief and of anger. Of disbelief. She watched as the body was loaded into the back of the anatomist's wagon. Watched as the coachman leapt back into the box seat and goaded the horses into a trot, and the wagon disappearing around the corner.

Grace rushed forward, snatching her father's arm before he could disappear into the jail.

"How could you!" she cried. "How could you!" She swung her fists, raining blow after blow against his chest. Wild sobs tore through her. Never in her life had she felt more betrayed. She had spent so many years defending her father, convincing herself – and anyone else who would listen – he was a good and decent man. She had helped him keep prisoners calm when he had felt unable to do so. Had covered up the paint on the front door early in the morning to prevent him from seeing it. And yet here he was, selling the body of her beloved to pay off debts racked up at the gambling halls.

Llewellyn stood motionless for several moments, letting her take her anger out on him. Finally, he gripped her shoulders, forcing her into stillness.

Grace gulped down her tears. "What have you

done?" she managed, her voice coming out strained. "How could you?" And then, her voice breaking, she coughed, "I trusted you."

Llewellyn blinked back tears of his own. He reached into his pocket and handed Grace a folded piece of paper. "Gracie," he began before his eyes overflowed. He wiped his eyes with the back of his hand. "I'm sorry for everything, my love. I know you don't understand everything that's happened lately. But soon you will." He nodded at the piece of paper. "I need you to go to the address on this page."

Grace frowned, opening the paper to see an address in Kensington scrawled in her father's messy handwriting. She sniffed. "What's this about, Papa?"

Llewellyn swallowed heavily. "You'll see soon enough." He pulled her suddenly into his arms and held her tightly. "I love you, Grace," he said. "More than you could know. And I'm so sorry for everything." He kissed the top of her head.

Grace stepped back, looking up at her father. Her thoughts were knocking together. She wanted to hate her father and was still furious over what he had done to Phillip. But his tears tore inside her. What was he not telling her?

"Please, Papa," she pushed, "just tell me what this is all about. Why did you sell Phillip's body to the anatomist?" The words made her voice waver again.

Llewellyn cleared his throat and met her eyes. "The address, Grace." He gripped her shoulders. "I need you to go there. Right now. Promise me. It's very important."

Grace stood with her lips parted for a moment, questions on the tip of her tongue. But finally she just nodded, tucking the piece of paper into her pocket. Then she turned and left the jail, without speaking to her father again.

GRACE SAT in the back of the cab, wringing her hands. She shifted impatiently on the bench seat as the city crawled past the window.

She had no idea what she would find when she reached the address on the paper. But her father's insistence had worked its way beneath her skin. Though she had no thought of what was awaiting her, she was tremendously impatient to get there.

Answers, she hoped, were what she would find. A reason for her father having been so distant these past few days, when she had needed him so.

And yes, a part of her was hoping for some justification for his selling Phillip's body, although she knew she would never find such a thing. Not even the threat of poverty was enough of a reason for him to do such a thing. She had thought her father had known that.

But Grace was beginning to wonder whether she had ever known her father at all.

After what felt like an eternity, the carriage rolled to a stop. "We're here, miss," the coachman called. He opened the door and offered her a hand.

Grace looked up at the enormous house before her. It was an imposing white mansion with rows of wide oriel windows and hedges lining the front fence. A narrow path cut through a neat garden, leading to the front steps.

Grace glanced down at the paper in her hand. Had she made a mistake? Had the coachman brought her to the wrong house? But no, this was the address her father had scrawled down. This was the place he had been so eager for her to visit.

She couldn't make sense of it. But then, she hadn't been able to make sense of much that had happened over the past few days.

Smoothing her skirts and tucking a stray strand of hair beneath her bonnet, Grace walked slowly up the front steps. She felt out of place amidst such finery. Drawing in her breath, she lifted the brass knocker and knocked three times.

At once, footsteps sounded down the passage and a butler answered, dressed in a neat black suit.

"You must be Miss Dillingham."

Grace frowned. "You were expecting me?"

The butler gave a short nod. "Yes, miss. If you'll come this way." He set off at a brisk pace, his shoes clicking rhythmically on the flagstones of the enormous foyer. Grace hurried after him, her gaze darting at the rows of gold-framed portraits hanging on the wall. A wide spiral staircase reached up to the second storey and beyond. The butler led her into a hallway lined with doors on either side. He stopped outside one and knocked lightly.

"Yes?" called a man's voice from inside.

"Miss Dillingham, sir."

"Very good. Show her in."

The butler opened the door to reveal an older, grey-haired man sitting at a large oak desk. Papers were spread out in front of him, along with a large inkpot and a steaming mug of what smelled like coffee. Behind him, enormous windows looked out over the vast lawn behind the house. The man stood up as Grace entered. He came towards her slowly, offering her a smile. He was tall and well dressed in a silk shirt and embroidered waistcoat. "Miss Dillingham. Come in, please. Sit down." He gestured to a chair beside his desk.

She peered uncertainly around the room, before perching on the edge of the chair. "What's all this about? Who are you?"

"My name is Stephen Walker," the man told her. "I'm an anatomist. I—"

"An anatomist?" Grace's lips parted. "You're the man my father sold the bodies to." She heard her voice rise involuntarily. "Phillip. Where is he? Has he been brought here? What will you do with him?" She leapt to her feet, suddenly overwhelmed with anger. Why would her father have sent her here of all places? What had he been thinking?

She strode up to Walker's desk and slammed her palm down hard. "You can't have him, do you understand? He's to be buried at Saint Mary's beside his father where he belongs!" Tears began to sting her eyes. "He's an innocent man. He deserves a real burial."

Walker held up a hand in a gesture Grace assumed was intended to calm her. "Miss Dillingham, please. I will explain everything. Sit down, please."

"I'll not sit down," she hissed.

To her surprise, the anatomist's lips curled into a small smile. "As you wish." He strode over to a door connecting his study to an antechamber. He pulled it open and peered into the next room.

"Mr Butler? There's someone here to see you."

*Mr Butler?* The anatomist's words made Grace begin to tremble. Was this all some kind of sick joke? Her thoughts were racing wildly. Footsteps sounded across the antechamber. And in an instant, Grace's every thought fell away as Phillip stepped out into the anatomist's office.

## CHAPTER 17

*G*race stared in disbelief. This was an illusion, surely. This was her grieving mind playing tricks. It had to be. She felt hot and dizzy. Felt the world around her swim. She grabbed the edge of the desk in a desperate attempt to steady herself. Phillip lurched hurriedly towards her, grabbing her arm before she fell. His grip was warm, firm and achingly real. She stared up at him, hardly daring to believe it.

"Tell me you're real," she gushed, her tears overflowing. She pressed her palms to his cheeks. "Tell me I'm not dreaming."

Phillip's face broke into a broad smile. "I'm real, Gracie. You're not dreaming."

Grace let out a sob of joy and rushed forward,

throwing her arms around his neck. How was this possible? She had watched Phillip die. Not a single part of this made any sense. But right now, she didn't care. The man she thought she had lost was holding her in his arms, and that was all that mattered.

She took a step back, taking him in as she let her tears flow freely. There was the fading bruise beneath his eye and the cut on his cheek that he had received in prison. But he was otherwise unharmed. Whole.

Alive.

She gripped his hands, her eyes darting between Phillip and the anatomist. "How is this possible?" she managed. Her thoughts were tangled, her mind racing. But a blinding joy engulfed her.

Mr Walker gestured to her chair. "Perhaps you might sit down?"

Grace nodded shakily, finally accepting the anatomist's offer to sit. Phillip perched on the chair beside hers, not releasing his grip on her hand.

The anatomist turned to Phillip. "Mr Butler? I believe you're better placed to tell Miss Dillingham exactly what eventuated. How it is you came to be here."

"This was my father's doing," Grace said before either of the men could speak again. She didn't understand how he had done it or what had taken place. But there was suddenly no doubt in her mind that Llewellyn had been responsible.

Phillip nodded. "Yes. The plan was his from the beginning."

*FOUR DAYS earlier*

LLEWELLYN LAY ON HIS SIDE, staring at the thin threads of dawn peeking through the curtains. He had not managed a minute of sleep. Nor, he guessed, had Grace. How could she when the man she loved had just been sentenced to death?

Throughout the night, he had heard her sobbing intermittently, her cries broken by restless footsteps as she padded back and forth across her bedroom.

On more than one occasion, Llewellyn had thought to go to her. Hold her in his arms like he used to do when she was a girl, and tell her every-thing would be all right.

But of course, nothing would be all right. Not only was Phillip to die, he was to do so at her own father's hand. And Llewellyn felt instinctively that he was the last person Grace wanted to see.

He could not let Phillip die. Though Llewellyn had no thought of how he might stop the hanging, he knew he had to find a way. This, he told himself, would be his way of making up for all the lives he had taken. All the lives he had destroyed.

Because, as much as Llewellyn tried to tell himself he was only doing his job according to the court's determining, the fact remained that he was the one who took men's lives. People's lives.

How many people? He had kept count in the early days, in those first years before his marriage when he had been determined to scratch out a decent living. Keeping count had felt somehow respectful; a way of ensuring those lives he took were never forgotten. But there were too many now. Too many names, too many crimes, too many faces. Most of them blurred together, though there were several he knew would always stand out.

The first prisoner he'd killed: a hunched and bitter man in his fifties who had stolen a fortune from his employer. When he had walked to the scaffold that day, Llewellyn had been sure his heart was pounding as hard as the condemned man's. Over and over, he had told himself he was doing his job. Told himself that the man deserved to die. He barely remembered the execution. But he remembered that afterwards he had felt nothing. Just a faint sense of satisfaction that he had done his job as required.

Then there was the prisoner who had first made him question it all: a man convicted of murder who had proclaimed his innocence right onto the gallows. That had been the first time Llewellyn had felt a reluctance to pull the lever. The first time he had imagined walking away and refusing to do his job. But he knew, of course, that he could never do so. He was to bend to the law like the rest of them. In a way, he was as powerless as the prisoners standing beside him on the scaffold.

The three women he had put to death last year were also faces he would never forget. But he knew that nothing would ever stay with him as deeply as ending the life of Phillip Butler.

Though Llewellyn tried not to dwell on it, he knew his role as a hangman had played the main role in his wife's suicide. His role as an executioner had destroyed his family. He would not let it destroy Grace's life any more than it had already. Somehow, he would find a way to not be powerless.

He had lain awake all night, thoughts turning over, searching for a way to save Phillip from the scaffold. And now, with the first hint of dawn beginning to lighten the room, Llewellyn could also feel the first threads of a plan beginning to form.

Exhausted though he was, Llewellyn climbed out of bed, splashing his face at the washbin to slough away the sleeplessness. He climbed into his shirt and trousers and then hurried out of the house before he crossed paths with Grace.

AFTER ALMOST TWENTY years of putting prisoners to death at Stepney Prison, Llewellyn was beginning to hate the place. No, he thought, he had felt hatred for the place before. On more than one occasion. He had certainly hated it when he had walked these cold stone corridors on the day after his wife's death, with the knowledge that it had been his position that had sent her to her grave.

And he had hated the place when he had been tasked with putting those three women to death for the murder of their husband and father. He had hated the place then for his own inability to keep the women calm; had hated it when he had first seen Grace walking its halls. Stepney Prison was not a place he had ever wanted to see his daughter walk within. And now it was a place she was far too familiar with.

But while twenty years at Stepney Prison had given him so many terrible memories, it had also given him inside knowledge and a good relationship with the guards. And when he stopped outside a certain cell and demanded to be let inside, the guard opened the door without flinching.

The cell belonged to two brothers convicted of assault and robbery some days earlier. They had been sentenced to face the gallows on Friday, two days after Phillip was due to hang.

Llewellyn walked slowly into their cell, barely noticing the stench of waste and dirty skin that had become so familiar to him here. The brothers watched him for a moment without speaking, looking him up and down.

"Who are you?" asked one.

The brothers looked similar, with the same square jaw and thick, rust-coloured hair. He guessed the one who had spoken to be several years older than the other.

"My name is Llewellyn Dillingham," he told them. "I've been tasked with putting you both to death." He watched the men's jaws tighten, almost in tandem. Llewellyn held their gaze. "And I have a proposition for you."

The men glanced at each other. "What kind of proposition?"

Llewellyn swallowed. The moment he put this plan in motion, he was signing his own death warrant. But it didn't matter. He would die, but Phillip would live. And Grace would be happy.

"I will allow one of you to escape," he told the brothers. "And in exchange, the other will be hanged on Wednesday. Two days early."

The brothers exchanged glances again. "Why are you doing this?" asked the younger of the two.

Llewellyn shook his head. "That's not for you to know."

"And how do we know this is not some kind of sick joke?" asked the older brother.

Llewellyn let out a cold laugh. "What do you possibly have to lose?"

The brothers fell silent. Llewellyn could tell they knew he was right.

"Do we have a deal?" he asked.

Another glance between the brothers. Then the older nodded.

"Good," said Llewellyn. "You can expect me on Wednesday morning."

ON WEDNESDAY, Llewellyn was again up at dawn. He could hear Grace's bed creak loudly as she tossed and turned with sleeplessness. He felt his heart lurch. He could only imagine what she must be going through right now, on the morning she believed her beloved was to die. He longed to go to her and tell her everything. Comfort her, reassure her than soon her pain would be over and she would be back in Phillip's arms.

But Llewellyn knew there was no certainty his plan would succeed. How could he promise Grace she would have Phillip, only to take him from her again? No, Grace could know nothing of this plan. Not until it was over.

He couldn't pretend to be surprised when she insisted on coming to the execution. Though he had hoped to keep her away from the prison that day, he had always known it would be a battle he was to lose.

They rode to the prison in a silence Llewellyn barely noticed, his mind racing as he tried to cobble together backup plans and think through everything that could possibly go wrong.

The moment they arrived at the prison, he sent Grace to the execution yard. He needed her out of the way. He couldn't have her catch word of what he was planning – not yet. And he couldn't bear to see her and be reminded of all that was at stake.

When he stepped inside the prison, everything was quiet. It often felt this way before an execution. As though the building itself was holding its breath, waiting for Llewellyn to do his job. Waiting for the condemned to die.

As he approached the brothers' cell, Llewellyn reached into the pocket of his coat for one of the two whisky bottles he had brought with him that day. Payment for the guards. An incentive to turn the other way. He slipped the bottle from his pocket and held it out to the man guarding the cell.

"Open the door and don't ask questions."

The guard nodded wordlessly, pocketing the flask. He slid the key into the lock. It opened with a loud creak. The two brothers were on their feet, watching him with glowing eyes. He could see the fear on their faces. Fear that Llewellyn couldn't help but feel himself. If anything went wrong, if any of the guards chose to talk, he and Phillip would likely both end up on the scaffold. And where would Grace be then?

He cleared his throat. "Which of you is to die?" He could hear the brutality of his words, yet forced himself to keep his voice even.

The older brother stepped forward. "I am."

Llewellyn gave a short nod, then turned away, allowing the brothers a moment to say goodbye. How had they reached such a dreadful decision, he wondered. Had they simply drawn lots? Or had the elder man sacrificed his life for his brother?

Llewellyn shook the thought away. He couldn't afford to dwell on it. He had learnt early on that the best way to cope as a hangman was to not get drawn into who his victims were as people.

When he turned back to face the men, the older brother's jaw was set grimly, the younger man with his eyes fixed to the filthy floor of the cell.

He led the elder brother down the passage towards the condemned cell, sliding the second whisky bottle from his pocket and handing it to the guard at the door. Into the cell he and the older brother went, with no questions asked.

He found Phillip pacing back and forth, arms wrapped around himself and his eyes wide with fear. He looked up at Llewellyn in surprise.

"Mr Dillingham? Is it time already?" His voice was thin.

"No, Phillip," said Llewellyn. "It's not. But I need you to come with me. And don't ask questions."

Phillip nodded obediently.

Llewellyn turned to the older brother. "Thank you," he said. "I'll see that your brother gets to safety. And I'll see that…" he swallowed, "you don't suffer." Why were those words getting harder and harder to say?

He turned away from the condemned man, unable to look him in the eye. And he led Phillip down the passage and into the brothers' cell.

"What's happening, Mr Dillingham?" Phillip whispered once the cell door had locked behind them.

Llewellyn looked between Phillip and the younger of the brothers. "I'll see to it that you both escape the prison tomorrow morning. You must be awake and ready to leave at dawn." He turned to

Phillip. "And if anyone ventures into this cell, you must hide your face. For this ruse to work, everyone must believe you were hanged today."

Out of the corner of his eye, Llewellyn could see the younger brother close his eyes. Could see the realisation that his brother was about to be sent to the scaffold in Phillip's place. Llewellyn looked away.

He knew with certainty that this would be his last execution. He could not return to this place after this ruse. And nor did he want to.

Without speaking again, he left the two men in the cell and made his way towards his small office. On the other side of the prison gates, he could hear the crowd gathering in the execution yard for Phillip's hanging. Grace, he knew, would be among them. What would it do to her to watch the man she loved die? Not for the first time, Llewellyn wished there was a way to tell her of the plan he had put in motion. But no. Not yet. Grace would find out soon enough.

Llewellyn took the two black hoods that hung on a hook beside the door and made his way back towards the condemned cell. He pulled the first hood over his head and then stepped into the cell and handed the second to the prisoner.

"You must wear this now," he said. "The guards will lead you to the scaffold. And no one must see your face."

GRACE LET OUT HER BREATH. How could she have dared think the worst of her father? How could she for a second have imagined him capable of selling Phillip's body? She felt a deep pang of guilt.

"So you were kept in the brothers' cell," said Grace. "While the older brother was hanged in your place."

Phillip nodded. Grace thought back to the way the condemned man had been led from the prison with his hood already in place. At the time, she had assumed it was her father's doing; had assumed he had insisted on Phillip wearing the hood so that she might be spared seeing his face as he was about to die. But now she saw the truth. Llewellyn had insisted on the condemned man wearing the hood in order to hide his identity.

Grace closed her eyes for a moment, trying to process all she had just learnt. If there was one thing she was certain of, it was that she would never doubt her father again.

"This morning your father came to the cell where I was hiding," Phillip continued. "He told the younger brother and me that Mr Walker's carriage was waiting outside the jail. We were taken from the prison grounds together with the older brother's body."

Grace's lips parted. "You were at the prison this morning? You were there when…"

"When you confronted your father," Phillip finished. "Yes."

Grace let out her breath. She could hardly make sense of it. While she had been staring at the anatomist's carriage, silently cursing her father, Phillip had been right there, crawling into the back of the coach, about to find his way back to her.

He shifted forward on his chair and squeezed her hands. "I wanted nothing more than to climb from the carriage right then and there, Gracie. To tell you I was alive. I couldn't bear to see what all this had done to you."

"I know you couldn't have done such a thing," she said gently. "If anyone had seen you…" She dived suddenly into his arms again. "Oh, Phillip. I can't believe you're really here. I'm so afraid I'm going to wake up and this will all be a dream." She sat back in her chair and turned to look up at the anatomist. She had thought the worst of him when she had first learned who he was. But how could she continue to do such a thing when he had helped to save Phillip's life?

"Thank you, Mr Walker," she said. "For everything."

He nodded. "Of course. I've known your father for many years, Miss Dillingham. I know he's not always had it easy, and I know him as a good and decent man. When he told me about Mr Butler's situation, I told him I would do all I could to help. I only regret you all had to suffer so much in order to get here."

Grace gave him a small smile. Right now, with Phillip's hand in hers, that suffering felt like a distant memory.

Mr Walker shifted on his chair, his face darkening suddenly.

"I regret that the two of you are not safe here, Miss Dillingham," he told her. "Wrongly convicted or not, the fact remains that Mr Butler is an escaped prisoner."

Grace's breath left her. In the joy of finding Phillip alive, she had not stopped to consider the implications of all that had taken place. Of course, they could not just return to their old lives.

Phillip's house and business had been forfeited to the Crown. And the city still knew him as a murderer.

"Where are we to go?" she asked.

"I promised your father I would have my coachman take you outside the city," said Walker. "After that, you must find your own way. Take on new identities. Build a new life."

Grace's heart began to quicken. New identities? Build a new life? She glanced at Phillip. His face was stony, but he did not look afraid. Just resolute. They had no choice, Grace realised. If they wanted a life together, they had no choice but to disappear from London and start afresh. After a moment, she dared to ask, "What of my father?"

A heavy silence pressed down on the room. Grace felt Phillip's fingers tighten around hers.

"I'm sorry, my love," Phillip said quietly. "It's only a matter of time before the authorities find out what he did. The two brothers are due to be hanged tomorrow. And the prison will discover then that your father allowed one to escape. If they haven't done so already."

Grace's stomach turned over. "And then?" she managed. But she did not need to hear the answer. She knew well what would happen to her father when the authorities discovered he had let two prisoners go free. He would walk onto the same scaffold on which he had ended so many lives.

"No." Grace shook her head emphatically. "No. We have to go back for him. He can come with us. He can…" But she faded out, knowing the futility of it. She thought back to the tearful farewell her father had given her that morning when he had sent her off to the anatomist's house. At the time, she had assumed his tears had come from guilt. But now she saw. They were the tears of a father who knew he would never see his daughter again. The tears of a man who knew his time was almost up.

She squeezed her eyes closed, feeling grief well up inside her. She had only just got Phillip back, and now she was to lose her father? She could hardly believe that life could be so cruel.

Phillip knelt at her feet, covering her hands with both of his. "I'm sorry, Grace. I truly am. But he was determined to do this. He wanted you to have a good life. He wanted us to be happy together."

Grace nodded through her tears. She had no doubt of that. All Llewellyn had ever wanted was for his daughter to be happy.

"This is all Drake's fault," she coughed. "If it weren't for him, you and I would be married, and my father would be safe and..." She trailed off, overcome by tears. Phillip held her tightly, saying nothing.

The anatomist's chair squeaked as he got to his feet. "I'm sorry, Miss Dillingham, Mr Butler. We really ought to leave. The longer we delay your escape, the more danger you will be in."

Phillip climbed to his feet. "Of course." He tugged Grace up with him, sliding an arm around her. "Come on," he said gently. "It's time to go."

GRACE AND PHILLIP sat huddled together in the back of the anatomist's wagon, feeling the carriage lurch as it rattled over the cobblestones. The inside of the windowless coach was almost pitch black with just a thin seam of light straining through the gap in the door. She tried not to think of all the dead bodies that had been crammed into this carriage to be carted off to the Barber Surgeon's Hall. She felt herself shuffle closer to Phillip at the thought.

She tried to imagine the streets they were rattling down. Streets she knew so well, and that she would likely never see again. She thought of her empty home, thought of Phillip's townhouse and the property agency he had poured so much of his time into. They had no choice but to leave it all behind. London was the only home she had ever known. The thought of starting afresh filled her with anxiety. How were they to manage? How was she to manage without her father? The thought of Llewellyn's sacrifice brought a fresh ache to her chest. Phillip pressed a kiss into her cheek.

"I love you," he murmured. Grace pulled him close, pressing her head into his shoulder.

"I love you, too." And at once Grace knew that whatever lay ahead of them, they would manage, just as long as they were together.

AFTER WHAT FELT LIKE HOURS, the carriage slowed to a halt. Grace heard the thud of boots on stone as the coachman leapt from the box seat. He pulled open the back of the wagon, causing her and Phillip to squint at the sudden stream of light.

"This is it," he told them. "This is as far as I'm going."

Phillip slid out of the wagon, holding out his hand to help Grace out behind him.

"Where are we?" he asked.

"Just on the edge of Watford." The coachman pointed to a large stone building on the corner. "That's the Royal Hotel. A coach leaves from there that'll take you as far as Liverpool."

"Liverpool," Grace repeated, taking a step closer to Phillip and reaching for his hand.

The coachman nodded briskly. "Good luck to you."

Phillip shook his hand. "Thank you for everything."

Grace murmured her thanks and then watched after the coach as it began to roll back toward the city. Her heart quickened as it disappeared around a corner. The uncertainty of what was next was overwhelming.

She looked up at Phillip. "What are we to do?" she asked. "We've not a penny to our names."

Phillip reached into his pocket and produced a leather pouch. He handed it to Grace. "Your father gave me this earlier this morning," he told her. "Said it was for the two of us. To help us start our new life."

Grace opened the pouch and peered inside. It was heavy with coin and bundles of rolled notes. She let out her breath as she thought of the two men hauling their belongings out of the house. "This is from the sale of the furniture."

"And the house," said Phillip. "He got much less than it was worth, but he made the sale quickly."

Grace closed her eyes. "He knew he wouldn't be coming home." Two fresh tears slid down her cheek and she pushed them away. "He gave everything he had so we might have a new life."

Her father had sacrificed himself so that she and Phillip might be happy together. And Grace was determined not to let him down.

## CHAPTER 18

Grace slung the wet washing over the line at the back of the cottage and peered up at the cloud-drenched white sky. The warmth of summer had given way to cold autumn days. She rubbed her wet fingers together to warm them.

With the empty washing basket pressed to her hip, Grace made her way back into the small stone cottage she and Phillip now called home.

The morning after the anatomist's assistant had deposited them in Watford, they had taken the coach to Liverpool. Two weeks later they had used the money from the sale of the house to purchase their new home in Bootle, close to where the Mersey entered the Irish Sea.

They had married a few days after arriving, in a tiny ceremony at would now be their local church. As she'd stood at the altar, gripping Phillip's hands, Grace had thought back to the wedding day she had envisaged; walking down the aisle at Saint Mary's in her blue silk dress, clutching her father's arm. It was a stark reminder that life rarely went the way one planned. And yet, as she looked into the eyes of the man she loved – the man she had been so certain she had lost – she had felt nothing but overwhelming gratitude.

Phillip, now going by the name of John, had found work at the shipyards, building vessels that were to sail the world. It was a tough and physical way to earn a living, a far different existence to the life of bookkeeping and property sales he had lived in London. But every day as he left the house and every day he returned home to her, Grace could see a light in his eyes. A look that told her he was just happy to be alive.

Though their new life was a happy one, thoughts of Llewellyn were always at the back of Grace's mind. She had not heard a word from her father, of course, and she knew she never would. Neither had any idea where the other was. Grace knew she would never hear from him again. It was just the way he had intended it; a way to keep her and Phillip safe.

And there, beside the memories of her father, were darker, more vicious thoughts. There was that consuming anger at Drake Matthews. That burning need to see justice done. An anger that even nights wrapped in Phillip's arms were unable to wash away.

Grace set the washing basket down in the laundry and made her way to the kitchen to prepare supper. Thoughts of Drake were gnawing at her. What was he doing now, she wondered. Was he prowling the streets for pockets to pick or drinking in the Fox and Hound Tavern with the members of his gang? Men he would not hesitate to kill for his own gain. She tried to shake the thought away. She didn't want Drake Matthews to have a place in her new life.

She picked up one of the potatoes in front of her and began to hack at the peel. She was glad to hear the front door creak open. Glad to hear Phillip's even footsteps sounding down the hallway. He appeared at the door of the kitchen and watched her attack the vegetables.

He came towards her slowly, putting a soft hand to her shoulder. Pressed a gentle kiss to the edge of her lips. The beard he had grown to disguise himself tickled her skin, and she could smell the sea on him. "What are you thinking?" He sat in a chair beside her and lifted the knife from her hand.

Grace stared blankly into the pile of discarded potato peels. "I'm thinking of Drake," she admitted.

Phillip reached for her hand and tugged her down into the chair beside him. "Why?"

"Because," she said, "there's no justice to any of this. You and I have been forced to leave the lives we once knew. You lost your business, your home. I lost my father. All because of Drake's need for revenge. All the while, he's going about his life with no consequences, happy as he ever was."

Phillip didn't speak at once. He laced his fingers through hers. "Do you really imagine Drake Matthews is happy?" he asked finally. "He's been seeking revenge since he was a child."

Grace hesitated. He was right, she realised. Even at eight years old, Drake had been black-eyed and bitter, determined to seek revenge for his father's death. She wasn't sure she had ever seen a genuine smile from him; at least not a smile that didn't come from enjoying another's misfortune.

"You think that punishment enough?" she asked. "That he is going about his life unhappy?"

Phillip shrugged. "I don't know, Grace. Who are we to decide what punishment a man deserves?"

Grace closed her eyes for a moment. The words reminded her of the things she had said to her father after the women's execution on the night they had discussed the rights and wrongs of putting criminals to death. She nodded faintly. "Perhaps you're right."

"In any case," said Phillip, his hand tightening around hers, "I didn't think I'd live to see today. And I didn't think I'd live to make you my wife. Whatever else has happened, we've been given a second chance. And I refuse to let Drake Matthews ruin that."

Grace leant forward, leaning her forehead against his. "I know. You're right. For that I will always be grateful." She looked down at the newspaper folded on his knees. "What's that?"

She watched something pass over Phillip's eyes. Something that made her stomach roll. "Phillip? What's happened?" She heard her voice rise.

Phillip held it out to her. "I'm sorry, Grace," he said. "I'm so sorry."

Sick rose in Grace's throat. For a second, her vision blurred and the letters swam across the page. But there was the headline, in big, bold letters:

*Condemned hangman hanged.* She couldn't pretend to be surprised by this. She had known it was coming. But that did not help the grief welling up inside her. She took the paper and laid it out carefully on the kitchen table.

Phillip touched her shoulder gently. "There's no need to read it all, Gracie, I just thought—"

"Yes," she said. "There is. I need to read it. Every word." Her voice wavered. "Everything my father did, he did for me. For us."

Phillip nodded in understanding. He sat silently back in the chair, sliding a gentle hand up and down her back.

Blinking back her tears, Grace looked down at the page. *Llewellyn Dillingham, hangman at Stepney Prison, was arrested last Saturday outside the Globe Tavern in Whitechapel...* The article spoke of how her father had allowed two prisoners to escape before their execution. His motives remained unknown. Grace's tears overflowed and she pushed them away hurriedly, forcing herself to keep reading.

*Sources confirm Mr Dillingham's home was sold for cash on the day after the prisoners' escape. The whereabouts of his daughter, Grace, are unknown.*

The final paragraph was the most difficult. Her father, Grace read, had been hanged by William Calcraft at Newgate. Over ten thousand people had been in attendance.

Grace turned suddenly and buried her head against Phillip's chest. He held her tightly, stroking her hair. Had had her father walked to his death calmly, she wondered. Had he been dignified and composed, just like all the prisoners he had helped throughout his career? Yes, she thought. She was sure of it. A calm death was something Llewellyn Dillingham had always believed was of utmost importance. She knew his own would have been nothing but dignified, even despite William Calcraft's crowd-pleasing theatrics.

After a moment, Phillip took a step back, bending his head a little to look her in the eyes. "Are you all right?"

Grace coughed down her tears, nodding slightly. The grief was there, of course. Violent and overwhelming. And yet a tiny part of her felt relief. She had known for the past month that her father's death was coming. Knew he was going about his days in dread, waiting for the law to catch up with him. Waiting for death to find him. She hoped he was now at peace.

Phillip took her hand. "Come with me." He led her into their bedroom and opened the drawer of his side table. He pulled out a folded piece of paper with her name scrawled on the outside. Grace recognised her father's handwriting. The sight of it drew a violent sob from her. Phillip handed her the letter.

"Your father gave me this on the day he helped me escape," he said gently. "He made me promise not to give it to you until after his death."

Phillip climbed to his feet and kissed her gently on the forehead. "I'll leave you to read it," he said. "I'll be just outside."

Grace nodded, clutching the paper between her hands. For a long time, she just sat, staring down at the unopened letter. This felt like the last piece of her father. She wanted to preserve these last words, wanted to leave them unread for as long as she could. But she also needed to hear what he had to say.

Finally, she drew in a long breath and unfolded the letter.

*My dear Grace,*

*I am so proud of you and the woman you have become. I know your mother would be so proud of you too.*

As she read, Grace could hear Llewellyn's voice in her head, speaking to her gently in his deep gravelly voice. Tears blurred the page and she blinked them away, forcing herself to keep reading.

*I know it has been no easy thing for you to have a father who does what he does. A father who takes others' lives for a living. It was a great challenge for your mother, and believe me when I say it has been a great challenge for me too. I believe you were right when you said that the power to choose whether one lives or dies should not lie with man.*

*But this dreadful role I have played throughout my life has given me the opportunity to do some good. To help an innocent man escape. To help my beloved daughter have the life she deserves. For this, I will always be grateful.*

*I will die for the things I have done, I know this well. But please do not be sad for me, Gracie. I am ready and willing to die, for it means I will be reunited with the woman I love. I have many regrets, but this sacrifice is not one of them.*

*I wish you every happiness with Phillip. I know you*

*will have a long and happy life together, and as I face my own death, I am comforted by this fact.*

*I know I have not always been there when you needed me, and I know I have not always been the father I ought to have been. I only hope that you can forgive me. I hope there will always be a place for me in your heart.*

*With all my love*

*Papa*

Grace let her tears slide from her cheeks. One spilt onto the page, blurring the ink. She squeezed the letter tightly between her fingers, holding it against her chest.

"I forgive you, Papa," she murmured. "I love you." And at that moment, all thoughts of Drake Matthews fell away. All thoughts of revenge, of seeking justice. After all her father had done for her, she could not let her life be consumed with thoughts of that sad, bitter young man. She owed it to Llewellyn to be happy. To make him proud.

And that was exactly what she was determined to do.

"*A*nd finally,*"* Grace said, her voice rising with enthusiasm, "I urge you to ask yourselves whether this is the future we want for our children. Do we want them to live in a world where innocent men and women are put to death? Where people are punished with their lives for suffering the fate of poverty? Or do we want them to live in a world where the power to choose if a man lives or dies lies only with God?"

The crowd huddled around the small wooden dais, broke from their hush and erupted into applause.

"Well said!" shouted a man at the back of the crowd.

Grace felt a smile on the edge of her lips. The

crowd had almost doubled in size since the last time she had stood here in the town square and shared her views on the death penalty. The movement was gaining momentum, though not as quickly as she had hoped. Perhaps true change was still far off. Perhaps there would be many years of men standing on the scaffold as hangmen, and carrying their guilt on their shoulders each day they left their families to go to work. But perhaps if she continued speaking, continued gathering people to her cause, one day that might change.

Though this was a cause she fervently believed in and had done for so much of her life, she had been nervous to speak out at first. Nervous of speaking her mind in front of strangers, yes, especially when her views ran contrary to the beliefs of so many people. But she had also been afraid of being recognised. Afraid a London police officer might have found his way to Liverpool. Might catch sight of her husband and send him back to the gallows.

But Phillip had reassured her. "It's been almost three years since we left London. And not once has anyone questioned us or shown any sign of suspicion. We're well hidden. We've left our old life behind." He had squeezed her hands tightly. "You ought to do this," he had said. "I know it's what your father would want."

Grace was thinking of Llewellyn as she looked out over the crowd who were now chattering excitedly among themselves. This was what he would have wanted, she thought. She felt sure of it. How proud it would make him to see his daughter standing up in front of a crowd like this and speaking of the things she believed in.

As she made her way down the steps at the back of the dais, a man dressed in a dark greatcoat and peaked cap came hurrying towards her. Judging by the notepad and pencil in his hand, Grace assumed he was a journalist.

"A word, perhaps, Mrs…"

"Cooper," said Grace. "Mary Cooper."

"Can you tell me why this cause is so important to you, Mrs Cooper?" the journalist asked, pencil poised. "You speak so passionately about the subject, it feels as though it is personal."

For a moment, Grace longed to speak of her father. Longed to tell the world what a fine and decent man Llewellyn Dillingham had been. But of course, she could do no such thing. In this new life, she was Mary Cooper, wife of a shipyard worker, and outspoken advocate for an end to the death penalty.

And so she said simply, "Yes, I have been touched by this issue on more than one occasion."

She thought suddenly of Drake Matthews. It had been many months since he had worked his way into her thoughts. Her life in Liverpool was so busy, so happy, that there was little room in her mind for the dark and bitter Drake. Perhaps one day the law would find him and his men, she thought to herself. Perhaps one day they would be punished. But whatever happened to Drake, she realised she didn't care.

"Mama!" Grace looked away from the journalist to see her son toddling towards her. His little arms were outstretched, red curls poking out the sides of his knitted cap. Grace smiled to herself, swinging him into her arms.

In a second, Phillip was at her side.

"Forgive the interruption," he puffed. "Can hardly keep up with him these days. Caught sight of his mother and he was off like a shot."

Grace laughed. She turned to the journalist. "My husband, John. And my son, Llewellyn."

The journalist shook Phillip's hand and tickled

Llewellyn under the chin. "A fine family you have, Mrs Cooper."

Grace smiled. She took a step closer to her husband, enjoying the feel of his shoulder pressed against hers. Llewellyn wriggled in her arms.

"Thank you," Grace told the journalist. "I come from a fine family myself. And I'm very pleased to carry on the tradition."

THE END

Printed in Great Britain
by Amazon

63214314R00163